# Salazar's Angels of Death

Miguel Araújo Oliveira was born in Hamburg in 1979. He is the author of several monographs featuring writers such as John Dos Passos, Günter Grass, and Ödön von Horváth. Ever since the launch of Oliveira's collection of poetry, *Sem Título*, he has been considered a major figure in present-day Madeiran literature. A selection of his poems was included in several anthologies of contemporary Portuguese poets. Oliveira has been invited to teach as a professor at several universities in Lisbon.

# Salazar's Angels of Death

## A Tragedy in Two Farces

Miguel Araújo Oliveira

Bibliographic information of the German National Library:
The German National Library lists this publication in the German
National Bibliography; detailed bibliographic data is available on the
Internet at dnb.dnb.de.

The original Portuguese edition of this play was published in 2017
under the title *O PIDE*. The first German-language translation was
published in 2021 and was republished in 2024. The English translation
is based on the German version.
Publisher: BoD • Books on Demand GmbH, In de Tarpen 42, 22848 Norderstedt
Print: Libri Plureos GmbH, Friedensallee 273, 22763 Hamburg
ISBN: 978-3-7597-9700-1

for Melanie and Nicole

---

to the victims
*in Memoriam*

»For it shall not be forgotten
in the mouth of their descendants«
(Deuteronomy 31:21)

# Content

# Dramatis Personæ

»I have called thee by thy name«

(Isaiah 43:1)

**Guilherme Vasconcelos** Student at the Faculty of Law at the University of Lisbon

**Rafael Eduardo Barros** Student at the Institute of Economics and Finance at the Technical University of Lisbon

**Manuel Fernandes e Castro** The accused

**Noémia Cardoso** Friend of Ana Luísa Rebelo and a student at the Institute of Economics and Finance at the Technical University of Lisbon

**Maria Correia Costa** Mother of Pedro Miguel Costa

**Jorge Henrique de Sousa** Friend of Cláudio Pestana

**Ana Luísa Rebelo** Death victim of the secret police DGS

9

| | |
|---|---|
| **Pedro Miguel Costa** | Deportee to the penal colony of Tarrafal, Cape Verde |
| **Cláudio Pestana** | Prisoner in the dungeon of Caxias of the secret police DGS |
| **Priest** | |
| **First Agent** | DGS |
| **Second Agent** | DGS |
| **António João dos Ramos** | Police officer |
| **Criminal Judge** | At the Boa-Hora court of justice |
| **Maria Amália Ramalhos** | Mother of Rafael Eduardo Barros |

# First Farce

## First Scene
»The Truth...«

*It is April 10, 1974, in the middle of the night. We are in a room in the Tribunal da Boa Hora[1] where a small group of dissidents, mostly students, have broken in. The entrance and exit are on the left side of the stage. On the same side, facing the audience, is a judge's bench. In the center is an empty desk. There are four chairs on the right-hand side of the stage. The stage light falls on the judge's bench and the chairs.*

[*All the dissidents are dressed discreetly. Noémia Cardoso sits on one of the chairs on the right side of the stage. Guilherme Vasconcelos, a student at the faculty of law, sits at the judge's bench. He looks concerned and worried. The atmosphere is tense. Maria Correia Costa is walking back and forth nervously. The silence is almost unbearable and weighs heavily on everyone in the room.*]

**GUILHERME VASCONCELOS** [*upset*: — Damn! Sit down! Your ups and downs are getting on my nerves! [*Restrains himself*: — Pardon me, please! I just got carried away!

[*Maria Correia Costa, a woman in her mid-fifties wearing a dark skirt, looks at him in dismay. Obediently, she sits down on one of the empty chairs. She looks at her watch. Time passes. Nothing happens. Only now and again does a nervous clearing of the throat by Guilherme Vasconcelos interrupt the silence. Suddenly, a noise can be heard from outside. Rafael Eduardo Barros and Jorge Henrique de Sousa enter the courtroom. They push Manuel Fernandes e Castro into the room. Manuel's face and upper body are covered with a brown, robust potato sack. His hands are tied behind his back.*]

**GUILHERME VASCONCELOS** — Finally! -- Has anyone seen you?

**RAFAEL EDUARDO BARROS** — No! – I'm pretty sure! No one did. -

**GUILHERME VASCONCELOS** — Take that off him!

[*Jorge Henrique de Sousa removes the potato sack off Manuel Fernandes e Castro's head. Rafael Eduardo Barros assists him. They then remove the rope with which they had tied Manuel's hands. Manuel Fernandes is led to the desk in the center: the dock.*]

**MANUEL FERNANDES E CASTRO** — Where am I? What is this?

[*Manuel Fernandes looks anxiously around. He looks at everyone's face. Suddenly, he runs for the exit and tries to escape. But Rafael Eduardo Barros grabs his arm just in time. Jorge Henrique de Sousa comes to his aid. Together, they defeat Manuel Fernandes. They forcibly bring him back to the table and sit him down roughly on the chair. Intimidated, Manuel Fernandes stops resisting.*]

**MANUEL FERNANDES E CASTRO** [*protests:* — What do you want from me? Who are you? What's this all about?

**GUILHERME VASCONCELOS** — Shut up! We're asking the questions here! Do you understand?

[*Manuel doesn't answer. From behind, Rafael Eduardo Barros hits Manuel on the head.*]

**GUILHERME VASCONCELOS** — Do you understand?

**MANUEL FERNANDES E CASTRO** — Yes, I do! --- I do understand!

[*Guilherme signals to Rafael Eduardo Barros and Jorge Henrique de Sousa to sit down. Manuel follows them with a frightened look.*]

**GUILHERME VASCONCELOS** — What's your name?

**MANUEL FERNANDES E CASTRO** [*in a shaky voice*: — Manuel e Castro.

**GUILHERME VASCONCELOS** — Manuel Fernandes e Castro! Right?

**MANUEL FERNANDES E CASTRO** — Yes, Manuel Fernandes...

**GUILHERME VASCONCELOS** — And you don't know why you're here today? You have no clue at all why you might be here?

**MANUEL FERNANDES E CASTRO** — I don't know! I don't even know where I am!

[*Rafael Eduardo Barros laughs out. It's an evil laugh.*]

**GUILHERME VASCONCELOS** [*disdainfully*: — Oh, you don't know where you are? -- You really don't know? Why don't you take a look around? You've been here before, haven't you? [*Convinced*: — Even more than once! --- You're here in the Tribunal da Boa Hora! Does that mean anything to you?

[*Manuel Fernandes shakes his head. Another evil laugh from Rafael Eduardo Barros.*]

**GUILHERME VASCONCELOS** [*sarcastically*: — Of course not! --- Do you know a young woman called --- Ana Luísa?

**MANUEL FERNANDES E CASTRO** — No! --- I've never heard of someone called -- Ana Luísa. --- No!

**GUILHERME VASCONCELOS** — Ana Luísa ... Rebelo! --- Are you sure you never knew her? I have a picture of her here!

[*He gets up and brings the photo to Manuel Fernandes e Castro, who is sitting in the dock. Guilherme puts the photo onto the table, right in front of Manuel Fernandes e Castro.*]

**GUILHERME VASCONCELOS** — So you don't recognize her?

[*Manuel looks at the photo with wide, open eyes. He is still frightened. He shakes his head.*]

**MANUEL FERNANDES E CASTRO** — No! I don't know her! --- What's this all about? Why...

**GUILHERME VASCONCELOS** [*gruffly shouts at him:* — Shut up! I've already told you! I'm the one asking the questions!

[*Rafael Eduardo Barros stands up. --- Guilherme gestures for him to sit down again.*]

**GUILHERME VASCONCELOS** — And Cláudio Pestana?

[*Pause.*]

**GUILHERME VASCONCELOS** — Jorge Henrique de Sousa?

[*Pause.*]

**GUILHERME VASCONCELOS** — Pedro Miguel Costa?

[*Pause.*]

**GUILHERME VASCONCELOS** [*full of contempt*: — You don't know them either, do you? --

**MANUEL FERNANDES E CASTRO** — No! I don't know these people. None of them! I've never heard those names in my life!

**GUILHERME VASCONCELOS** — Well, well! You don't remember the names! Maybe you'll remember them when you see their faces? --- Maybe then you'll remember something!?

[*Guilherme puts more photos on the table. Spreads them out. At first, Manuel doesn't want to see them. Furious, Guilherme grabs Manuel, bends him over abruptly so that Manuel's nose lands on the photographs. Guilherme finally lets go of Manuel. Manuel is looking at all the photos now. Frightened. Trembling. He shakes his head.*]

**MANUEL FERNANDES E CASTRO** — No, I swear! I don't know them! I've never seen them before!

**JORGE HENRIQUE DE SOUSA** — Liar! But of course, that bastard knows me!

[*Manuel Fernandes turns around to Jorge. Looks at him. Shakes his head again.*]

**MANUEL FERNANDES E CASTRO** [*desperately*: — I swear I don't know them! Not him, and not the others either! I swear it, by my blessed mother!

**RAFAEL EDUARDO BARROS** — Son of a bitch!

**NOÉMIA CARDOSO** — Murderer!

**MANUEL FERNANDES E CASTRO** [*wailing*: — I... a murderer? --- [*Desperately*: — I've never seen them before! I swear, by God, I don't know them!

**GUILHERME VASCONCELOS** — That's odd! There are people here who swear that you knew them. And

15

that you knew them all. All of them, without exception! --- But that's why we're here today – to find out the truth!

[*Guilherme returns to the judge's bench.*]

**GUILHERME VASCONCELOS** — I declare this trial session open! Manuel Fernandes e Castro is accused of being a confidential informer of the PIDE.[2]

**MANUEL FERNANDES E CASTRO** [*protests:* — Me? A CI? I've never worked for state security!

**GUILHERME VASCONCELOS** — Shut up! Don't interrupt me! --- This is my last warning!

[*Manuel Fernandes e Castro looks around again, intimidated.*]

**GUILHERME VASCONCELOS** — ... Accused of being a collaborator of the PIDE and of denouncing our friends and fellow students from my faculty and others! To find out the truth, this court calls the first witness: --- Noémia Cardoso!

**MANUEL FERNANDES E CASTRO** — I beg your pardon? I must protest! What kind of court? This must be a bad joke! By what authority? What do you think you're doing? I refuse to recognize this court! I do not acknowledge it! This is a silly boy's prank! Nothing else! A vile prank!

**GUILHERME VASCONCELOS** — That's enough!

[*Guilherme Vasconcelos gives a wave to Rafael Eduardo Barros, who immediately gets up and walks towards Manuel.*]

**MANUEL FERNANDES E CASTRO** [*stands up:* — Let me out of here! You'll regret this tasteless hoax! I promise you that! --- We can still forget this whole business now. I won't turn you in either!

[*Rafael Eduardo Barros punches Manuel Fernandes e Castro in the jaw. The blow is so hard that Manuel's nose bleeds. Rafael Eduardo Barros forces Manuel to sit down again. Manuel offers no further resistance. He takes a handkerchief out of his pocket and tries to dab the blood. Guilherme signals to Rafael Eduardo Barros to sit down again.*]

**GUILHERME VASCONCELOS** [*unimpressed, as if nothing had happened*: — Miss Noémia Cardoso! --- Please come forward!

[*Noémia Cardoso, a young woman, stands up. She stands next to Guilherme at the judge's desk.*]

**GUILHERME VASCONCELOS** — Do you swear to tell the truth, the truth, and nothing but the truth?

**NOÉMIA CARDOSO** — I swear, Your Honor!

**MANUEL FERNANDES E CASTRO** [*between his teeth*: — Don't make me laugh! Your Honor!

**GUILHERME VASCONCELOS** [*ignoring him*: — Please! You hold the floor!

**NOÉMIA CARDOSO** — Ana and I -- Ana Luísa Rebelo, we're both studying economics and financial management. -- On February 23 we were both walking down the Marquis de Fronteira Street. Just as we were about to pass the Henrique Mendonça Palace,[3] I saw a man standing on the other side of the street pointing at Ana. Two men in civilian clothes then approached us. They asked us our names, and we answered them. One of them immediately grabbed Ana by the arm and said it was better not to make a fuss and to follow him. They

17

would just ask her a few questions, and then Ana could go home. Ana didn't resist and went with him. I don't know where they went.

[*Pause.*]

**NOÉMIA CARDOSO** — The other one asked me for my address. I was afraid. So I told him where I lived. It was better that way. Because he made me go home right away. He accompanied me to the front door. From then on, a man in plain clothes watched the house. Whenever I went out, whether to university or just to a café, whenever I went for a walk or to an appointment, they followed me. Sometimes they were already there. Pretending to read the newspaper as if nothing was wrong. They were waiting for me. I sat down --- listlessly --- and looked at them, sometimes scornfully, sometimes devastated.

[*Pause.*]

**NOÉMIA CARDOSO** — Whenever I returned home, I found the drawers on my desk half open. At first, I wondered if I had actually left them open before I left the house. Out of sheer carelessness. But when I examined the desk more closely, I realized that someone must have gone through my correspondence. Letters that had previously been in closed envelopes had been opened! The pages in my address book seemed slightly crumpled at the edges. My clothes, which had been hanging neatly and ironed in the wardrobe, had suddenly become wrinkled here and there. Some blouses had even fallen off the hanger. I watched carefully to see if anything on the shelves or pieces of furniture had been moved. I looked around nervously to see if anything else had been stolen from me apart from my inner peace. [*Hysterically.* — Whoever had gained access also searched my bed. They checked to see if there was anything hidden under the mattress. If something was under the sheets or the pillow. They turned over every rug! They inspected my photos on the bedside table. They probably removed them from the frames. Besides, they must have gone through my dirty laundry. The rubbish bin. They must have inspected my food in the kitchen. Who knows... if they didn't spit in it?! --- And in the bathroom... There were fingerprints. On the mirror cabinet that weren't mine. [*Grabbing her head.* — Or were they mine, and I'm just imagining things? --- What if they had used the toilet... What if they had used my soap to wash their hands like Pilate!? --- Oh, that's disgusting! -- I no longer felt comfortable within my own four walls! I could no longer wash myself. Lie down. Sleep. --- I even stopped answering the phone. Making calls. Who knows if they weren't bugging my phone? --- There were days... when I went through all the books on my shelf very thoroughly. One after the other. I was afraid they'd put a forbidden title there. From Marx. Lenin. Trotsky.[4] Just so they could foist it on me and arrest me. ---

[*Pause.*]

**NOÉMIA CARDOSO** — Once, they even forgot to lock my front door again behind them. They just left it ajar. Without the latch snapping into the door lock. I was so angry. Because anyone could have gotten into my flat in the meantime! --- Another time, it was humid weather, they had opened a window. And left it open! -- You could ask yourself whether they were amateurs, downright bunglers at work. But they weren't dilettantes! None of this was by accident. They wanted to let me know. Unequivocally! They wanted me to know that they could come in and out of my house whenever they wanted. As they pleased. --- Food was suddenly missing from the kitchen. They had made sandwiches and eaten them at my house. Because there were breadcrumbs everywhere. Scattered on the carpets. Scattered in the living room. In the hallway. Even on my bedsheets. Then, once, they left a note on the bread bin. It was written very legibly that I should keep cheese and sausage in the house for my guests. Just butter would be too bland for them. ---- It seemed to give them sadistic pleasure. To take away my peace and quiet. To rob me of it. To break me. To wear me down. To trample on my nerves. To surrender me to the madness - the persecution mania - completely.

[*She falters briefly. Breathes shallowly. Gasps for air. Air!*]

**NOÉMIA CARDOSO** — At some point, I thought about calling the police. The PIDE was offending me. By trespassing. I wanted to report to the police that I had been wronged. But what good would that have done? After all, it was the PIDE, the state security service, that had me spied on. The police wouldn't have lifted a finger for me. On the contrary. It would have been much more likely for them to eagerly support their colleagues from state security in their surveillance of my home. Or they would have gotten me for slander. And beaten me up. --- But who else could I have called to free me from this horrible feeling of impotence? I would only have exposed my friends and family to danger. - I was desperate! Out of fear, I didn't confide in anyone. I kept quiet. But I so desperately needed to talk to someone. With Ana, for instance... --- I almost went mad. I almost lost my mind... Because my illusion that I could feel safe within my own four walls was shattered into a thousand pieces. Into a thousand shards of clay that I could count night after night. Like others count sheep. I count shards of life: one, two, three, a hundred, a thousand fragments...

[*Pause.*]

**NOÉMIA CARDOSO** [*sighs with relief.* — But one day -- they lost interest in me. - Thank God! They let me back into my life. Even to this day, I haven't been able to regain my inner peace. --- The PIDE thought it was more important to send their henchmen out to inspect the posters on the notice boards at the university. I watched them take notes on the content of the posters. How they recorded our protest and our indignation in writing. Our rebellion. They recorded it in detail. Our aversion, which was hidden between the lines of the hangouts. Against the dictatorship. Against the repression. Against the tyranny and exploitation of the factory workers. – I've seen them take down and tear up the poster just because it had a battered woman in a Vietnamese straw hat on it. They know only too well what this picture stands for! The armed conflict in Vietnam. Against which we are clandestinely demonstrating. --- [*Takes a breath*: — Yes, they let me back into my life. -- Thank goodness!

[*Pause.*]

**NOÉMIA CARDOSO** [*worried again*: — But we never heard from Ana again. Not even her parents have been informed of what has happened to her since. She's still missing today. Maybe they just put her in prison! Or maybe she was murdered? -- The uncertainty is unbearable![5]

**GUILHERME VASCONCELOS** — So it was a man who denounced Ana Luísa Rebelo?

**NOÉMIA CARDOSO** — Yes!

**GUILHERME VASCONCELOS** — Was it the accused?

**NOÉMIA CARDOSO** [*thoughtfully*: — He certainly resembles him! I saw him from a distance. --- I took just a glance. And I was afraid. I immediately looked away. --- And it was a long time ago. --- Still...

**MANUEL FERNANDES E CASTRO** [*pale*: — Certainly? Alike? How could that be if it wasn't me! It wasn't me! It's not my fault that I look like a man who denounced you and your friend!

[*Rafael Eduardo Barros stands up and assumes a threatening stance.*]

**RAFAEL EDUARDO BARROS** — Shut your mouth, henchman!

[*He looks expectantly at Guilherme Vasconcelos, but Guilherme shakes his head. Rafael Eduardo Barros sits down again.*]

**GUILHERME VASCONCELOS** — Do you know where Ana Luísa is? Do you know if she's still alive?

**MANUEL FERNANDES E CASTRO** — I don't know anything!

**GUILHERME VASCONCELOS** — Why did you denounce Ana Luísa Rebelo?

**MANUEL FERNANDES E CASTRO** — I've already said that I didn't denounce her! I don't even know her! How can I denounce someone I don't know?

**NOÉMIA CARDOSO** — Ana was denounced because she stood up for the emancipation of women! Why should we study if we are neither allowed to work with equal rights nor taken seriously in our fields of study? Today's women, the modern women, are still not given a place in politics, society, or the economy. This must change!

**MANUEL FERNANDES E CASTRO** [*laughs maliciously, then remarks seriously:* — Where a cock crows, there's no soup hen to cluck! Emancipation, you've got to be kidding me...

**NOÉMIA CARDOSO** [*interrupts him brusquely:* — As we all know, Ana was denounced because, she was a women's rights activist, as well as a member of the Communist Party! - Ana was denounced because she

23

publicly supported the strike in January, when the miners were fighting for a pay raise and better working conditions! Ana loudly condemned the death of Júlio Pinto, one of the miners who was killed during the repression of the strike.[6] It's clearly political reasons that explain her denunciation!

[*Uneasily, Rafael Eduardo Barros whispers something to Jorge Henrique de Sousa.*]

**MANUEL FERNANDES E CASTRO** — What do I have to do with all this hullabaloo? Didn't your friend know that it's dangerous to belong to a banned party? To take part in strikes or demonstrations against the government? That she would one day be denounced by whomever because of it? --- I only know one thing: it wasn't me! I didn't denounce anyone!

[*Pause.*]

**NOÉMIA CARDOSO** [*foxy:* — The more I see you sitting there self-righteously, the more I'm convinced that it was you! Yes, you! You just want to get away with it! You, who speak so disparagingly of other people's desire for freedom and equality! You condemn us at any sacrifice! You are the real criminals! You stooges of the PIDE! How much did you get for Ana Luísa's life? Judas! How much did you get paid for your treason?

**MANUEL FERNANDES E CASTRO** — I haven't received anything from anyone! I have already said, and I say again, that it wasn't me! I don't even know her, this Ana! --- I, a criminal? What kind of accusation is that? What kind of trial is this? What right do you

24

think you have? You're acting against the law here! Not me! You kidnapped me! It's you who are holding me here against my will! Without any legality! You have no warrant for my arrest! It's not a police authority that has ordered my arrest! You want to do justice with your own hands, and you don't realize that you're only dirtying them! With what malice do you talk about justice? Is nothing sacred to you? Law and justice are the responsibility of the state! Not you!

**GUILHERME VASCONCELOS** — Justice. What about fairness? In this country, justice is neither just nor fair! It intimidates the truth! The law only serves a few! Those who are more equal before the law than others. More equal than the people! That's why we have to take matters into our own hands! --- So that justice can still be served! ---

**RAFAEL EDUARDO BARROS** — Blessed are those who hunger and thirst for justice, for they will be satisfied today!

**MANUEL FERNANDES E CASTRO** — Hurray, what a bunch of heroes do I have before me! --- Who have you brought to my defense? In this country, there's a defense lawyer in every court to make sure...

**RAFAEL EDUARDO BARROS** [*gruffly interrupts him*: — Make sure you're hanged!

[*Laughter.*]

**MANUEL FERNANDES E CASTRO** — What kind of double moral standard is this?

[*Rafael Eduardo Barros stands up.*]

**RAFAEL EDUARDO BARROS** — Look who's talking about morality!

[*More laughter. Rafael Eduardo Barros takes his seat again.*]

**GUILHERME VASCONCELOS** — Enough! --- If you want a defense lawyer, we will provide you with one. I ask all those to raise their arms who wish to assist the accused as counsel!

[*No one answers. Only after some time does Noémia Cardoso carefully raise her arm.*]

**MANUEL FERNANDES E CASTRO** — Are you joking? You've all conspired against me here. And now [*mockingly:* — Your Honor says he'll appoint someone from among you rags to defend me!

**NOÉMIA CARDOSO** [*hatefully:* — Rags? Don't judge others by yourself! You're in cahoots with the regime! You are the very worst, and then you have the nerve to call us rags? You do the PIDE's reputation full justice!

**MANUEL FERNANDES E CASTRO** — Enough of this hogwash! Then why don't you name the hero here in my defense who just physically attacked me! That's all I need! If this isn't a bad joke, then what is it? Would one of you really defend me? In whose interest? In the interest of the accused or the prosecution? I demand an unbiased defense! Not a legal defense bought by you, poisoned, and compromised by your malice and lies! That is perfidious! I'm not a snitch! I'm not a henchman, but an honest and blameless citizen!

26

**GUILHERME VASCONCELOS** — That's enough! -- I assure you that Miss Noémia Cardoso, who is here today, is just as partial or impartial as any other defense lawyer serving in our courts today! -- Do you want a defense lawyer or not?

**MANUEL FERNANDES E CASTRO** — No, thank you! I'll do without! I won't give in to the wolf in sheep's clothing! Those who are innocent have nothing to fear! [*Shouts*: — And I have nothing to fear! --- And this is not a court case! This is pure nonsense. Nonsense! I don't have to defend myself against your accusations! This is all absurd! Leave me alone now! Let me go! Right now!

**GUILHERME VASCONCELOS** [*indifferent*: — Mrs. Maria Correia Costa!

[*Maria Correia Costa, who has stenographed everything that has been said so far, gets up from her seat.*]

**GUILHERME VASCONCELOS** — Please write down that the defendant has waived his legitimate right to legal representation, which would have been granted to him by this court. Also note that he considers himself innocent!

[*Maria Correia Costa sits down again and begins to write down what she was dictated.*]

**GUILHERME VASCONCELOS** — Thank you very much, Miss Noémia Cardoso! You may step down.

[*Noémia Cardoso takes her seat again on the right side of the stage.*]

**GUILHERME VASCONCELOS** — I call Maria Correia Costa, the mother of Pedro Miguel Costa, to the stand!

[*Maria Correia Costa stands up. She hands her notepad to Noémia Cardoso. Maria Correia Costa walks towards Guilherme Vasconcelos and meets the accused, whom she looks penetratingly and firmly in the eyes. Then she looks away in disgust.*]

**GUILHERME VASCONCELOS** — Do you swear to tell the truth, only the truth, and nothing but the truth?
**MARIA CORREIA COSTA** — I swear!
**GUILHERME VASCONCELOS** — Please!
**MARIA CORREIA COSTA** [*takes a deep breath*: — My son was born in Angola. He came to Lisbon to study here. He was very aware of what was happening in the colonies and spoke out against the wars in Angola and Mozambique. He wrote a manifesto and distributed it. He distributed the leaflets in the center of the city. A few days later, there was a knock on the door at home. It was around four in the morning. Two agents in plain clothes entered. They came to pick him up. They took Pedro Miguel to António Maria Cardoso Street.[7] To the headquarters of the PIDE, where he was tortured. --- It wasn't until a whole month later that they let me talk to him. Only briefly. And only once. He told me... [*Her voice trails off*: — He told me that they interrogated him regularly. And whenever he didn't answer, they dunked his head into a tank of concrete filled to the brim with water...

[*Silence.*]

**MARIA CORREIA COSTA** — They ordered him to stand motionless, like a statue. This is a disgusting game by the PIDE. Their favorite pastime, my son told me. A form of torture. He had to stand stock-still for hours and was not allowed to move. Arms stretched out to the sides at shoulder height. Just like the savior, our Lord. Whenever my son lowered his arms, they'd beat him up. --- They beat him half dead! His eyes were swollen from the last beating they had given him. His face was... puffed up. [*She has to cry.*

[*Again, Rafael Eduardo Barros whispers something to Jorge Henrique de Sousa.*]

**MARIA CORREIA COSTA** — I brought the manifesto with me.

**GUILHERME VASCONCELOS** — Thank you! Can I ask you to read it out loud to us?!

[*Maria unfolds the manifesto.*]

**MARIA CORREIA COSTA** [*she proudly reads*: — Patriots! Brothers in arms! What does the dictatorship announce to us now? The government, in its arrogant attitude of dominance, decides to send more troops overseas to further isolate our country internationally. Instead of using the resources for the good of the nation,[8] the dictatorship decides on a military intervention so that we can burden ourselves with even more guilt. Comrades, our enemies are not the leaders of the independence movements in Angola and Mozambique! Our enemies are not the UNITA[9] or the FRELIMO![10] Our enemies are right here at home. They hole up in

29

their government buildings. But enough is enough! Away with these parasites! May the friends of our beloved fatherland now recognize their duty in this hour of utmost urgency! We must rise up! Fight fire with fire! Now is the time! On to the fight! Let's fight to undo the damage! Against oppression, imperialism, and capitalism! Against the subjugation, domination, and exploitation of the colonies! Against misery! Against the acute conflicts that torment our country! Let's free our country from the fascist plague of locusts! [*Raises her face full of patriotism, Maria knows the rest of the text by heart:* — Raise your faces and your hearts! Aim your weapons at the traitors! Comrades! Down with the dictatorship! Death to our enemies! The enemies of democracy! It's time to change the needle! The seam and the tailor! It's time to take off the steel thimble that is the PIDE! Long live the fatherland! Long live the Republic! God save the Republic! Freedom! God save the new, free culture! Decolonization! Democratization! The social and economic development of our country!

[*Rafael Eduardo Barros, Jorge Henrique de Sousa, and Noémia Cardoso stand and clap their hands. --- They sit down again. Maria Correia Costa folds the paper again and puts it in her pocket.*]

**MARIA CORREIA COSTA** — The case has been brought to trial. Pedro was identified as the distributor of the manifesto. However, they have not been able to prove that he wrote it. That's why he was released again. Pedro decided that remaining in

Lisbon wouldn't be safe. So he returned to Angola. But they were already waiting for him. When he arrived, he was intercepted at the port. He was arrested again and tortured. They wanted him to expose the author of the flyer. Of course, he didn't say anything. Eventually, he was deported. To the concentration camp of Chão Bom on Cape Verde.[11]

**GUILHERME VASCONCELOS** — Who testified against Pedro in court?

[*Maria Correia looks at the defendant with hatred.*]

**MARIA CORREIA COSTA** — I remember him all too well. His face! It's etched in my memory! The jet black hair. His full lips. The brown, suspicious eyes. The protruding chin. He was wearing a green turtleneck sweater. I won't forget it. The intense color of his sweater. --- It was him! That monster there!

[*Rafael Eduardo Barros, Jorge Henrique de Sousa, and Noémia Correia whisper something to each other in a somewhat muffled manner.*]

**MANUEL FERNANDES E CASTRO** — What nonsense!

**GUILHERME VASCONCELOS** — Thank you, Mrs. Costa! If you wish, you can take your seat again.

[*Maria Correia walks back to her seat, but as she passes Manuel Fernandes, she suddenly stops.*]

**MARIA CORREIA COSTA** — Do you know what it means to be a mother? Do you know what it's like to look into your own son's dead eyes? Do you know what it's like to hear your child screaming, even when he is far away? In Tarrafal? Well, I know what that's like! I hear his cries day and night! Cries of distress! Of despair! When he returns home and sits on the edge of my bed as a ghost. With big, puffy eyes. Completely white. White and full of fear. Too bloated to cry anymore. I don't know how he is. Whether he is okay or not. Not even if he's still alive! --- I don't want to think about it! Because I continue to harbor hopes of hearing from him one day! To be able to hold him in my arms again one day! My son! --- ---.

[*She pulls a handkerchief out of her pocket and wipes her tears with it.*]

**MARIA CORREIA COSTA** [*addressing the dissidents*: — He wrote me only one letter, which was opened by the censorship commission. Since then, he hasn't been allowed to write to me again. He is locked up in a cell, which he shares with criminals. Murderers and rapists! Among them, an innocent young man. My son! --- But what am I talking about? The prisons are overcrowded with innocent young people! Who have done nothing wrong![12] And among them is... [*almost inaudible and tired*: — my beloved son.

[*Turns to Guilherme and then back to the defendant.*]

**MARIA CORREIA COSTA** — If they let me, I'll scratch your face out, you pig! I'll rip your heart out of your chest, chop it into little pieces, and feed it to the first street dog I come across!

[*Manuel Fernandes stands up, unmoved. He is not afraid of women. Because, according to his worldview, they have no authority over him.*]

**MANUEL FERNANDES E CASTRO** — Because I, like so many other good citizens of this country, have black hair and brown eyes, this old, demented woman accuses me of being...

[*Maria hits him. Manuel Fernandes grabs her hands in anger.*]

**MARIA CORREIA COSTA** — He didn't respect my son! He branded him an outcast. But he will pay respect to this old, demented woman here and now! Yes, it was him! – This scoundrel! [*She frees herself from Manuel's grip and turns to the group:* — I swear to God! It was him!

**MANUEL FERNANDES E CASTRO** — You must be kidding me? Dear lady, you are just looking for a scapegoat! Someone you can condemn for your follies! But not with me! I am innocent! --- Lies! Nothing but lies! --- Comrades! Class warfare and similar nonsense. So you all want to be alike! But there is always someone who is more equal than the others! Always! While the Chinese ride bicycles, Mao Zedong drives a Rolls-Royce! Equality! Egalitarianism! Freedom! Please, don't make me laugh!

[*He sits down. Rafael Eduardo Barros stands up.*]

**RAFAEL EDUARDO BARROS** — The fool here is you! Not everyone who defends freedom has to be a communist or an anarchist! I am surely not!

**MANUEL FERNANDES E CASTRO** [*irritated*: — Freedom, freedom! It makes me sick to hear you talk about freedom as if it were a sacred cow! What do you know about freedom? It's chaos! Fornication! Decay! The end of society and the state! The Republic was a good example that the Portuguese don't know how to handle freedom! --- "There can be absolute authority, but never absolute freedom!"[13]

**RAFAEL EDUARDO BARROS** — No! It's people like you who don't know how to handle freedom! Because they just trample on freedom. The people want and need to be free! --- Just shut up! You're just getting yourself into hot waters right now, and you won't be able to get out of it safely! You are about to tie your own noose! On which you'll hang. ---- --- Long live the Republic!

**JORGE HENRIQUE DE SOUSA** — Long live the Republic!

**MANUEL FERNANDES E CASTRO** [*mockingly*: — Long live the Republic; don't go on like that! "We are a small country, with serious problems and must not join weak fronts just for the purpose of proclaiming that we are playing democracy!"[14] --- In your republic we will see "illiterate people in power, spoiled brats, fraudsters of all kinds," pimps, and crooks. "Most of them wouldn't even be suitable as servants, but they become mayors, representatives, managing directors, ministers, and even presidents of the republic."[15] The people are not mature enough to vote! They can't distinguish the honest from the fabulous, the hypocrites and the frauds! --- Ridiculous! A bunch of illiterates in the service of the nation!? Without any socio-political or economic competence... It was these grandiose figures who stuffed themselves during your holy republic and plunged the country into insignificance. --- They did nothing except enrich themselves! At the expense of the people. National debt, they have incurred nothing but debt! Since the end of the monarchy, forty-four governments have alternated in less than sixteen years. It was Salazar who, as a selfless servant of the fatherland, rescued Portugal from this utopian nightmare of freedom. It was the dictatorship under Salazar that made Portugal great again, restoring the country's stability, size, and prestige. That's the truth!

**RAFAEL EDUARDO BARROS** — Size and prestige? You probably mean megalomania! --- [*Teasingly*: — Selfless servant of the fatherland... Only a fool, a buffoon like you, can really believe this!

[*All dissidents laugh.*]

**MANUEL FERNANDES E CASTRO** — So I am a fool!? --- Just laugh while you can! You will soon see that a new republic, if it should be proclaimed, --- God forbid! --- would make Portugal dependent on the welfare and charity of other countries.[16]

**RAFAEL EDUARDO BARROS** — It seems as if we are currently living in clover.

[*All except Manuel Fernandes e Castro laugh again.*]

**MANUEL FERNANDES E CASTRO** — Aren't you? You're spoiled brats! All of you! You owe it to the dictatorship that you do not know what hunger is!

**RAFAEL EDUARDO BARROS** — Stupid chatter! You, the henchmen of the PIDE, are the ones who live on a grand scale. What do you know about hunger? What do you know about the conditions under which people in this country live and suffer? What do you care about their plight? You feast on it. How many pieces of silver do you earn from each report you submit?

**MANUEL FERNANDES E CASTRO** — I have never denounced anyone, but I will hand you all over to justice without payment --- without having to receive a single centavo![17]

[*The dissidents are getting restless. Guilherme Vasconcelos calls for order.*]

**GUILHERME VASCONCELOS** — Enough! That's enough!

[*Rafael Eduardo Barros sits down again.*]

**GUILHERME VASCONCELOS** [*addresses the accused*: — So you are still denying that you are an unofficial collaborator of the PIDE? Even though we have credible witnesses here who swear that on oath?

**MANUEL FERNANDES E CASTRO** — Credible? Don't make me laugh! Yes, I deny it! Because I am not! And anyone who claims otherwise must prove it! --- A green turtleneck!? Do I happen to have it on?

**MARIA CORREIA COSTA** [*cries out angrily and threateningly*: — Don't make a fool of yourself!

36

**MANUEL FERNANDES E CASTRO** — Maybe I have it hanging in my closet at home? Let's all go to my house! You're welcome! I invite you all to my home! But I'll save you the way and the work! I've never owned a green sweater before! --- I hate the color green!

**MARIA CORREIA COSTA** [*reproaching*: — Keep your sarcasm to yourself!

**MANUEL FERNANDES E CASTRO** — For the hundredth time: I've never had a green garment! Even less a turtleneck! I've never been to court! Not as a defendant! Not as a witness, and certainly not as an informer! I've had enough of this nonsense! I've had enough of your stupid accusations! Prove it was me! Where is your evidence? You want to convict me on the basis of false testimony! One liar says she can't swear it was me! She alleges that I have a few similarities with some guy. The other storyteller says that the man had black hair and brown eyes, just like I do! Just like many other citizens of this country! --- That's exasperating! Prove it! --- But you can't! Because you can only prove the truth! And I've told you the truth more than once! – Nonetheless, it is rather strange how easy it is to believe lies, to fall prey to them, and to prefer them to the truth.

**GUILHERME VASCONCELOS** — Our goal is to find out the truth, nothing but the truth! You declare yourself innocent, even though Mrs. Maria Correia Costa testified against you! Whose word is more credible than yours!

**MANUEL FERNANDES E CASTRO** — Is that going to start all over again? Will there never be an end to this? She's lying! It's her word against mine! I've never been in a courtroom, and I've never worn a green turtleneck! I've never reported or blackened anyone! But you can be sure that I will report you all! For this evil hoax.

[*Rafael Eduardo Barros laughs wickedly.*]

**MANUEL FERNANDES E CASTRO** — I'm not going to pull the chestnuts out of the fire for any of you! If you are on the edge of legality and sabotaging your homeland, it is definitely the duty of every patriot to come forward! So it is also my duty to report you to the authorities so that you can be held accountable for my abduction and maltreatment! For wanting to condemn me! Without having any legal recourse against me! I am blatantly accused of a crime that is not a crime! Denouncing the outcasts is a must! I don't get it, that you, who are mostly students, don't understand. There are still values and rules in this society that we have to respect and conserve, because otherwise we would drown in the mire! I don't understand your complaints! Isn't it this state that gave you the prerequisites and opportunities to study at university? What else do you want? How dare you criticize a government that gives you everything and more?

[*Rafael Eduardo Barros rises. But it is Maria Correia Costa who speaks.*]

**MARIA CORREIA COSTA** — You scum of humanity! You should be ashamed of yourself! What has this regime given us? Has it given us the freedom we seek? The highest good given to us by God and by nature, which we must defend at all costs!

**NOÉMIA CARDOSO** — Is it really your duty to send fellow citizens to their doom without any sense of guilt, just because they have different opinions? Knowing that a simple suspicion is enough to arrest them, torture them, and maybe even kill them?

[*Rafael Eduardo Barros rolls up his sleeves and steps forward.*]

**GUILHERME VASCONCELOS** — Calm down! Be quiet! We're not done yet! We haven't reached the end yet! Not even the verdict. [*Addresses the defendant*: — Yes, perhaps you are right! Homo homini lupus! Man is a wolf to man! However, it remains to be weighed up whether the current laws are really fair or even righteous!

**MANUEL FERNANDES E CASTRO** — You question if they are righteous? Who are you who dares to decide what is just and what is not? Is this tribunal just? It's a farce!

**RAFAEL EDUARDO BARROS** — But the fascist government knows what is fair and what is not?

**GUILHERME VASCONCELOS** — Enough talking! We have another case to deal with. Another eyewitness, wants to be heard! Wants to make his voice heard! Even if you don't want to hear it! Because you went deaf in both ears! I ask Jorge Henrique de Sousa to come here! To testify! To bear witness!

[*Rafael Eduardo Barros reluctantly sits down. Jorge Henrique de Sousa stands up. He joins Guilherme.*]

**GUILHERME VASCONCELOS** — Do you swear to tell the truth, only the truth, and nothing but the truth?

**JORGE HENRIQUE DE SOUSA** — I swear! So help me God!

[*Silence.*]

**JORGE HENRIQUE DE SOUSA** — Before I begin, I want you to know that I'm somewhat reticent about speaking to you! What I have to say is not easy. You yourselves could ostracize me. --- Cláudio Pestana was arrested and accused of passive homosexuality. He was tortured. He got to know the fortress of Peniche[18] inside out. They tortured him with a broomstick [*interrupts himself in embarrassment. After a short pause, he continues:* — and he was tortured with electric shocks on the genitals... He was sentenced to ten years in prison for kissing me on the mouth in public. It was on a corner near the Armazéns do Chiado.[19] We thought that no one would see us. But someone saw us. He spied on us! A few days later, they arrested Cláudio and took him to the fort. Under torture, they made him sign a confession of guilt, which was confirmed by a judge, who sentenced him to prison. He was put in a hole in Caxias.[20] A solitary oubliette. When I heard that they had arrested him, I immediately bought a ticket to Spain and left. I arrived in Madrid, from where I continued to Bilbao. Since I was afraid that someone might have followed me. I went into hiding with friends; who supported me in the most amiable way. Of course, with all the confusion, I had to abandon my law studies at the university. I am currently working on a construction site. I work as an apprentice bricklayer in the suburbs of the city. --- As a foreigner, I am assigned the dirty and most difficult work. Poorly paid, of course! But I don't want to complain... I manage to make ends meet, honestly. --- I have returned today because Guilherme sent me a letter, through trusted intermediaries, asking me to appear before this court. To testify and to identify the person who filed the complaint against Cláudio and me. --- My intention is to make my statement here and now and take the first train back to Spain tomorrow morning. I can't stay here... It's not safe here. --- Yes! It was him! Unlike Miss Cardoso, I am convinced! However, my word must serve as enough proof for you!

[*Silence.*]

**MANUEL FERNANDES E CASTRO** [*without any respect*: — Faggot! Gay pig!

[*Manuel Fernandes suddenly turns to the dissidents and stands up.*]

**MANUEL FERNANDES E CASTRO** — So this is the morality that you defend? That a man and a man may... together... with each other... --- disgusting! Disgusting!

[*He spits in the direction of Jorge Henrique de Sousa.*]

**MANUEL FERNANDES E CASTRO** — You all, tell me that you are not ashamed! [*Points to Jorge Henrique de Sousa*: — So this is what you are defending! Tell me if the torture wasn't used properly in this case? --- That's sick! That man and man... It's a disease! Unnatural. --- So, ladies and gentlemen, answer me! You and your beautiful morals!

**GUILHERME VASCONCELOS** — You want to come to us with morals? You who have no morals at all?! No country and no form of government should legitimize, let alone use, torture! Everyone must have the right to freely express their political or personal opinion. Everyone must have the right to live out their religious beliefs as well as their sexual orientation. It is true that Jorge has homoerotic preferences. Which we tolerate! We want others to tolerate our different ways of thinking, acting, living, and, yes, even loving! Our divergences and differences of opinion! According to Voltaire, who is the idol of our generation! --- But it is more than obvious that a PIDE does not understand this! You can't understand that Jorge's sexual life is neither my business nor yours! --- A PIDE like you...

**MANUEL FERNANDES E CASTRO** — PIDE, PIDE! Which PIDE? My God! I'll say it again: I've never worked for the state security service! --- And by the way, the PIDE doesn't even exist anymore!

**GUILHERME VASCONCELOS** — You don't have to take us for fools! For that, we have our mendacious press, which silences the truth! Honorable journalists: all of them are sufficiently beholden to the tentacles of power, united to distort the truth! The few honest journalists are subject to censorship or have been banned from their profession. According to the press, there is no unemployment, no poverty in our country. There are no strikes either. Nobody is committing suicide. Because the political and social distress that leads people to take their own lives is deliberately concealed from us. There are no demonstrations, even if we organize them. No crimes are committed. There are no accidents. There is no corruption. Once more, because all of the above are deliberately concealed from us. There is no food poisoning. There are no measles. No malignant diseases. There are no drug addicts injecting opioids. There is no domestic violence. Even the anti-Christ Nietzsche doesn't exist! By the time we get to read the articles, the censors have already cut them up. Cutting out the truth here and there. Do you seriously believe that if you are not allowed to write or speak publicly about the country's rampant problems, these problems will cease to exist? Out of sight, out of mind? --- The PIDE has changed its name. We know that only too well. Cheap propaganda! But state security was not abolished. The General Directorate for State Security, or DGS,[21] has the same powers as the PIDE once had. They wiretap us, torture us, kidnap us, and arrest us without ever bringing charges or bringing us before a court. The function of the DGS is still the same: to oppress the people! Just like the PIDE before it --- which learned to torture from the best: the National Socialist GESTAPO!

**MANUEL FERNANDES E CASTRO** — Nonsense! It's all rubbish! Lies! Your truth is degenerating into cheap gibberish for the free press! News is being sold! In the end, the truth walks the streets. There is a thin line between truth and falsehood. And this line will get thinner and thinner until you can hardly distinguish it anymore! -- Many thanks for the instructive words, too, dear Professor! You are quoting Voltaire from memory. And that everyone has a right to a free opinion. But you condemn my opinion! Yes, I am a Salazarist![22] And now what? Am I or am I not allowed to express this opinion in your republic? Which one of you wants to prevent me? You think you're better than this regime! You and your republic are not much fairer than the existing system! On the contrary!

[*Noémia Cardoso stands up.*]

**NOÉMIA CARDOSO** — It is curious, even demagogic, that you of all people should say that! Fascism doesn't allow us freedom of expression. No self-determination. But you have the insolence to insinuate, indeed to criticize, democracy for not allowing you to publicly advocate your malicious, right-wing populist ideology. You cry like a toddler and point your finger at blameless people. --- But to answer your question clearly: in a democracy, there is freedom of expression and the diversity of opinion that goes with it. This means that you are allowed to express your outrageous, perverted opinion, even if I can't stand it! But you will have to reckon with headwinds, counterarguments and corrections because freedom of opinion also means that lies must be exposed as such. Unlike under fascism, the people no longer bow to the opinions of the excellencies in power but meet them at eye level with their own point of view! That's why there will be no PIDE in our democracy, because you can freely say what you think!

**MANUEL FERNANDES E CASTRO** — I think you're clearly mistaken, you cheeky brat! There will always be state protection! Because even your looked-for democracy has tried to barricade itself behind paragraphs that enabled it, indeed guaranteed it, never to be abolished! Don't forget that censorship, which still restricts freedom of expression today, was introduced in your republic! You were not allowed to say everything, especially not during the First World War. Nobody was allowed to criticize Portugal's involvement against the German Empire. The seizure of German merchant ships docked in Portuguese harbors, which was ordered by your government, was ultimately responsible for the Germans declaring war on us!

**NOÉMIA CARDOSO** — Why don't you tell the truth? The government was pressurized by the British to seize German ships! --- But allow me a counter-question: are we allowed to protest against the colonial wars today?

**MANUEL FERNANDES E CASTRO** — No, of course not! I am also in favor of censorship! There will always be censorship. Even in democracy. Because it's necessary. To protect the state! For the good of the nation! Why don't you understand that?

**NOÉMIA CARDOSO** — You fascists are all the same! You have declared the people your enemy! But we want to represent the people with the democratic movement! We are the people! You only exploit the people! Your laws inflict punishment on the people! You shut us up because you don't want us to stir up your filth and show the public how corrupt you really are!

[*Noémia Cardoso takes her seat again.*]

**MANUEL FERNANDES E CASTRO** — To hell with your representation! I represent and defend the dictatorship! A strong state that rules with an iron fist! Let me finish! Now I'm talking, my friend! You have learned to read and write, yet in reality, you have remained illiterate! You all demand freedom of speech, even though you don't even know how to use it! You accuse us of corruption? That's ridiculous! Do you know what's wrong with democracy? The people elect a group of corrupt politicians to form a corrupt government. I remember the republic only too well! Promises and more empty promises they made! To capture the votes. Like the pied pipers. Once they were in power, they never kept any of their promises! Then suddenly, everyone started to lose their memory!

Amnesia. --- And now I wonder whether the state security you have just spoken of so disparagingly serves, as you say, to oppress people, or whether it does not serve to protect the rights of honest citizens! If the state security service were here now, they would protect me from you. You are nothing but terrorists! You dare to criticize secret court proceedings. And what are you doing to me here? Is this show trial open to the public or, in any way, legal?

**GUILHERME VASCONCELOS** — Serving the rights of honest citizens? Please don't make me laugh! Yes, of course! The interests of the state and co. You and your ilk have been talking a lot about the Marcelinist Spring,[23] celebrating it ever since your saint Salazar died. But the spring that his successor in office, Marcello Caetano, promised us remains a bleak, rainy autumn! But the days of freedom are within our grasp! In the name of justice, we demand the punishment of criminals and of murderers acting on behalf of the state! This trial here and now is only the prelude to our call for freedom, the struggle for freedom of an entire people! The fight of the courageous shepherd boy against the fearsome giant. David against Goliath. We are pronouncing the sentence that we will pass against you today on behalf of this very people. This is not a small, irrelevant trial against an insignificant individual like you. It is the first step. In the right direction. Towards democracy. Towards justice. Headed for freedom. This process is the dawn of a new era!

Against oppression and subjugation! Against the false news and the nationalist propaganda with which the government of the Estado Novo[24] inundates us every day and with which it seeks to declare us fools. Fools who should fall for their lies. But that's not the case! We have long since seen through them. This here and now is a trial against the system itself, against the assassins of the PIDE! It is time! High time! It is our time, which has now begun! The wind has changed. It blows fresh air into our faces. And awakens new vigor in us! We are now taking over the reins of our country's future and holding them in our hands! Of course, it will cost us dearly! Courage! Perhaps even our lives. Because the exploiters, cutthroats, and assassins will fight back. But it will do them no good in the end! When the people rise from their knees, throw off their bonds, their chains, and their shackles, not a stone will be left upon a stone! Not a head on the neck of the tyrants!

**MANUEL FERNANDES E CASTRO** [*bangs on the table*: — You are all mad! All I ever hear is freedom. Freedom! Do you know what you're saying? What patriotism are you displaying here? --- What are you preaching about a trial! What trial? -- You want to condemn me? Who are you, you snotty bastard, to judge me? Do it before a judge, before a public prosecutor! Who has to accuse me first! --- Someone who has the competence and authority to do so. Nothing else would be fair and legitimate! Nothing else serves justice! No matter how hard you try to justify your vigilante justice!

**GUILHERME VASCONCELOS** — Do you want to be tried by a judge? You are here in the honorable courtroom of the Tribunal da Boa Hora! A beautiful building! With beautiful ornamental tiles on the walls. This building claims to stand for morality and justice. But only a fool believes that justice will ever be done in this courtroom. The real culprits are never brought to justice. The little man, yes. He is brought to court when he steals a chicken and a few pennies to survive. The real Jacob, the one who has managed to evade the tax office and pocket hundreds of thousands of escudos,[25] is not in the dock of this court. You will find him well ensconced in his luxury property among all the wealth he has dishonestly snatched. And do you know why that is? Because it's easy to condemn a poor, innocent wretch. Blame him for the guilt of others. You can't put the real culprit, the rich man, in prison. No matter how corrupt he is! No matter how many crimes he committed! Even though his wealth stems from the exploitation and plundering of the working class and the state coffers. Because everyone benefits from the liberation of the rich! The lawyers. The corrupt judge. Even the government! No, in Portugal, there was never any danger of convicting a guilty man and making him atone for his guilt.

**MANUEL FERNANDES E CASTRO** — Oh, and you think it would be different in a democracy? --- Are you really that blinded? So naive?

49

**GUILHERME VASCONCELOS** — Are we supposed to be the naive ones here? Take a close look at the Federal Republic of Germany, which since the fall of the dictatorship, since 1945, to be precise, has been endeavoring to establish a democratic state with a separation of powers in the country. Neither the government nor the legislature influence the legal system. And the German economy has been flourishing since the mid-nineteen-fifties. The so-called economic miracle was no miracle at all; it was the result of freedom and the end of a totalitarian system!

**MANUEL FERNANDES E CASTRO** [*makes a throwing away gesture*: — Economic miracle... stories! You still believe in fairy tales! --- And do you think our dictatorship is total, urchin? Our dictatorship is authoritarian, yes! But it was never total! My Salazar was no Hitler! On the contrary! Salazar, in his great wisdom, kept us out of the world war – didn't he?

[*Manuel Fernandes e Castro sweeps the photos off the table with his arm. Rafael Eduardo Barros stands up.*]

**RAFAEL EDUARDO BARROS** — Fiddlesticks! Spare us your interpretation of history! Traitor! Angel of death![26] Our dictatorship created a monster: the PIDE, masterfully trained in misanthropy by Hitler's GESTAPO! --- What a fine service you are doing for us! Reporting innocent people? To blacken them. To denounce them. What crime have we committed? Is it an offense to be fed up with colonial wars? We don't want to go overseas, like my father, never to return! Because he was shot there in a senseless, injudicious war! We want to live in peace and without international embargoes? We want to be proud to be Portuguese again! Now that I can finally study, and only because my mother is sacrificing herself financially, saving on everything and on herself, I now have to fear that I will be mobilized at any time to serve in an ongoing and meaningless war. If you defend this regime of injustice, you are defending war! Why don't you go to war? Why don't you die in my place!? We don't need you here!

MANUEL FERNANDES E CASTRO — I...

[*Maria Correia Costa stands up.*]

**MARIA CORREIA COSTA** — You! Shut up, you bastard! Shut up, or we'll shut you up here and now! And for good!

**GUILHERME VASCONCELOS** — Please! Please stop it! Audiatur et altera pars! We have guaranteed him the right to defense! He has the right to be heard!

**RAFAEL EDUARDO BARROS** — He doesn't need any more rights! No more privileges!

**MANUEL FERNANDES E CASTRO** — In dubio pro reo! In doubt for the accused!

**RAFAEL EDUARDO BARROS** — Doubt? What doubts? There are no doubts! We know enough! We already know the truth! You made it clear to us that you are a fascist. And the fascists must be fought by using fire against fire and sword against sword! Every staunch supporter of fascism is morally a murderer! And to erase the guilt of a murderer, we must

become murderers ourselves. According to the millennia-old Talion principle, an eye for an eye! ---
**JORGE HENRIQUE DE SOUSA** and **MARIA CORREIA COSTA** [*in chorus*: — Murderer! Murderer!

[*Noémia Cardoso stands up. Asks for silence.*]

**NOÉMIA CARDOSO** — You've talked so much about the fatherland today. But what do you know about it? Why don't you explain to me, you know-it-all, what economic innovations the dictatorship has brought us? What economic investments have been made? In our capital city? In our economy and culture in general? We live in misery! In despair! And if you want to escape hunger, you have to emigrate! That's our human capital! Our emigrants out there! Their remittances. On whom we are financially dependent. We are condemned to gnaw on hunger cloth so that some who can't get their fill of the wall can live like kings in this country! My deepest needs cry out for freedom! For equality and justice! For I do not live by bread alone! You speak presumptuously and despotically of the fascist government! If the government were as good as you claim, it would fight poverty in this country instead of further exploiting and enslaving its own people! But what does the dictatorship do? Two students were arrested and sentenced to seven years in prison for daring to drink a toast to freedom in a café![27] Do you think that's fair? It's not a crime to demand freedom! But it is a crime to deny people their freedom! I'm not asking for much! I demand that we are all equal under the law and treated equally! Without distinction! May everyone have the right to freedom of expression and follow their conscience freely!

[*The dissidents applaud.*]

**MANUEL FERNANDES E CASTRO** — Are you talking about hunger? And has your beloved republic satiated anyone? Has freedom satiated anyone? Except your governors, their secretaries, state counselors, deputies, and mayors! Salazar died penniless! Without a single centavo in his pocket!

**NOÉMIA CARDOSO** — Who says so? The regime's propaganda! Did you have access to his bank account? --- Salazar could use the state coffers as he saw fit and for his own private purposes. – It seems the only one here who believes in fairy tales is you!

**MARIA CORREIA COSTA** — In your ranks, neither the blind nor the sighted see. Nor do the deaf hear, just as the hearing among your kind are unable to hear. Because you are all godforsaken! Blindly, you watch over your kin and cling to your rule. Silently, you obey your masters instead of listening to the needs of your people. You win one day and gamble away eternity. Paradise. This is your hour, since evil reigns. But soon the grain will be separated from the chaff! The good seed will sprout, and the weeds will be destroyed! You are the poison of the serpent that makes our mouths foam. You are the rigidity that has taken possession of us. --- But now it's over!

Enough is enough! Let's finally chase the devil away. Exorcise him at last!

**JORGE HENRIQUE DE SOUSA** — Yes! Enough now! Let's put an end to this! Let's put an end to this tragedy! So, --- what's the verdict?

[*Rafael Eduardo Barros responds with a theatrical gesture: he runs his thumb over his throat from left to right, implying the death penalty.*]

**RAFAEL EDUARDO BARROS** — Thus you shall give life for life, eye for eye, tooth for tooth, hand for hand, foot for foot, brand for brand, wound for wound, and weal for weal!

[*Manuel Fernandes looks desperately at Guilherme with a pleading look.*]

**MANUEL FERNANDES E CASTRO** — Fellas, don't do anything stupid! You don't know what you're doing! You can't...

**GUILHERME VASCONCELOS** [*interjects threateningly:* — You have no mercy to expect from me! You're whitewashing fascism and its atrocities! I am not the one who judged you! --- You have passed judgement yourself! In the name of the Portuguese people! Now, in the end, justice will be done!

[*Everyone gets up from their seats. Slowly. Manuel Fernandes screams desperately for help. But nobody comes to his aid. The dissidents laugh evilly. Manuel Fernandes tries to say something and stammers, but fear has overcome him and taken his voice.*]

**GUILHERME VASCONCELOS** — So far, you've been playing brave. But now, in the face of death, your knees are shaking. Now you finally realize your cowardice! --- Give to the emperor what is the emperor's!

[*Manuel Fernandes closes his eyes. The dissidents attack him. They attack the accused with all their might. Manuel Fernandes tries to flee again and again, but he can't escape the blows. At some point, his body falls to the ground. Maria Correia Costa scratches his face. The dissidents beat and kick Manuel Fernandes. Suddenly, you hear a thump from outside.* --- A man's voice comes out of nowhere, shouting: — Police! The building is surrounded! Surrender! *Everyone stops. Everybody looks in the same direction. Toward the stage entrance. Everyone slowly raises their arms. The defendant sighs with relief. Starts to laugh loudly. The laughter is spiteful and malevolent. The light dims. Goes out completely. Suddenly, there is new turmoil in the dark. Someone runs. Toward the stage door. A shot is fired in the dark. It echoes. A muffled scream falls to the ground. And only a moment later, a body slams hard, soon lifeless, onto the stage boards. More shots are fired. Echo. Echo... Until the hammer of the gun hits dry steel. Hammer. Hammer. --- Silence.*]

[*The curtain falls.*]

# Second scene

## »I have not come
## to call the righteous, but sinners«
### (Matthew 9:13)

[*In front of the curtain. Dim light falls on Ana Luísa Rebelo. The light gets brighter and brighter. She has a red carnation in her hand and is dressed all in white.*]

### ANA LUÍSA REBELO

— They've come to let me loose.
Out of the storeroom of memory.
Of the room that is denied to the living.
Where the dead do rest.
Where martyrs endure their deaths.
I am Ana Luísa Rebelo.
A member of the Portuguese Communist Party.
I was convicted,
without ever having been charged.
I am one of the victims.
Of this regime.
A victim of illness and abuse. ---
They fished my lifeless body
out of the icy, cold water of the Tagus River.[28]
The circumstances of my death
were quickly established.
Suicide, they said
the forensic experts,
who are not only in the service of the state,
but also in the service of repression.
The repression emanating from the state institutions
of the Estado Novo.

Suicide.
With the back of my head bashed in.

[*Pause.*]

## ANA LUÍSA REBELO

— Finally, my parents and friends --
were informed of my death. ---- A few days ago. -
I was taken into custody on February 23, 1974.
I was assigned a prisoner number.
That was carved on my skin.
2-7-4-5.
2-7-4-5 was tortured.
Was held at the mercy of the trained hands of the
secret police. ---
They smoked cigarettes.
Ordered me to put the lit cigarettes in my mouth.
To eat them. To swallow them --
while the ember ---- burnt my tongue.
They put out the burning cigarettes. On my back.
[*Ashamed*: — On my nipples
and on my pubic area.
Again and again.
They put their cigarettes out on my skin.
They put them out in the same spot. Just like before.
To make the pain unbearable to suffer.
They loved
to hear me scream.
Day after day. Night after night. ---- -
They put out... Put out their half-smoked cigarettes.
Always in the same place of skinless, burned flesh.
To cause me unspeakable pain.

They raped... [*her voice fails her.*
— This terrible, dreadful pain
that I endured
over and over again!
This appalling shame! This dishonor!
Until my agonized body,
finally, --- no longer bore
any more suffering.

[*Pause.*]

## ANA LUÍSA REBELO

— It didn't help,
to sing a song:
--- quietly ---
and with a shaky voice
[*hums the melody of one of the verses of the song
"A morte saiu à rua"
("Death takes to the road"[29]) by Zeca Afonso.*]
— Just to forget for a moment
to dismiss from my quiescent mind...
at least in my sleep
to put out the fire
out of my head
out of my scorching flesh...
Put out the turmoil,
with a song, with a thought of hope...
But after each new interrogation
I was more broken than before.
Was there one more burn...
Everything is so gloomy around here
in this tiny little cell...
and then...

suddenly...
[*With her arms crossed, she tries to cover her eyes*:
— The light! The horrible, glaring light!
With which they poke my eyes out.
Blind me ---
Whip me with the light. ---

[*Pause.*]

## ANA LUÍSA REBELO
— But I have not let go.
From my convictions!
I trust in victory! Of my ideals!
The working class will triumph!
That is the inevitable fate of our country!
For freedom!
To the end!
To the bitter end, if necessary.
It is.
Necessary.
For the communist movement!
To the bitter end!
For the laborers! For the proletarian! ----------------
----- To the end!
The end. -- Is near!
At last!

[*Pause.*]

## ANA LUÍSA REBELO
— You have struck my name from the book of the living.
I have let go of life.
They let my corpse into the water.

The river tore at my soul. Took it with him.
Into the depths.
I had descended. Into the realm of the dead.
Where it was dark. Bitterly cold.
When I slowly opened my eyes after the third crowing
and could see again, I saw a staircase. --
There was a white,
marbled staircase. In front of me.
The steps led skyward.
Upwards.
In front of the gates. Of Eden. ---
My mortal shell swam to shore. --
Someone has found it. ---

[*Pause.*]

## ANA LUÍSA REBELO

— The funeral was attended by friends. By the closest
family members.
And, of course, by the PIDE.
There were confrontations.
My uncle was beaten up.
They warned him. With the baton
they cautioned him.
By force, they convinced him.
To lay low.
He has two underage daughters.
You have to think about that. You have to
think twice.
[*She counts on her fingers*:
— Think. Think. –
Before you do something stupid.
Which you then regret. –

I regret nothing! Nothing!
I'm the last one to laugh! [*Laughs.*
*The laughter goes through the marrow.*
— Because here [*the light becomes whiter, divine-white,*
*glistening light falls on Ana:*
— In this realm,
I am light and love.
Here, I have found myself again!
Here, I have found peace and freedom.
Here, I have found God! ---
He will settle accounts with you.
This bill [*she points to herself:*
— will cost you dearly!
God is great! God is just!
God alone is righteous!
My blood will come upon you.
There is no water on earth
nor in heaven,
that could wash you clean.
In this judgement hall,
into which you will be led at the end of your life,
there is no corrupt judge.
There is no money in the world
that could wipe away your guilt here.
What you have sown, you will reap. ---
He will come to judge you:
to repay the living and the dead. Our dead. ---
Mine is the voice from the desert.
God is salvation!
Tomorrow, you will weep and gnash your teeth. -
We, the last, will be the first. --
It may be bewildering,

even strange,
to hear a communist talk about God like that!
Well, yes. Today, I know
that there is a God!
I was wrong. ---
Now I can remain silent.
Because the stones will cry out for me.

[*Ana Rebelo drops the carnation on the floor. She lowers her head. The light dims. Just before it goes out completely, Pedro Miguel comes on stage. He stands next to Ana. He also holds a red carnation in his hand. The light becomes brighter again until it shines completely on him.*]

### PEDRO MIGUEL COSTA
— I am Pedro. Pedro Miguel Costa.
I was deported to the Tarrafal labor camp.
A DGS labor camp.
On the island of Santiago.
In Cape Verde.
Where opposition members were originally sent to,
with the aim of removing them from the metropolis of
Lisbon.
And where the political prisoners from the colonies
are now being deported to.
I ended up here,
because I supported them.
The Marxist-Leninist
independence fighters.
From Angola and Mozambique. ---
I am tired. Tired of life.
Worn out.
The food is bad. Rotten.

They mix excrement into it.
The wardens urinate in the soup.
In front of us.
Just before they hand us.
The soup. Which we spoon up nonetheless.
Because we're hungry.
Then they laugh. Dirty. ---
It's hard bread.
Forced labor in the quarries.
We are marked and broken.
Exposed to the blazing sun
with our bare upper bodies.
The sun shines. From above.
My head is spinning,
when the tropical heat reaches its zenith.
At night, it's freezing cold.
That gets to me in the barracks.
And the solitude gnaws at me...
I desire so much
to socialize with the outside world
[*hoarse*: — to talk to my friends. Again.

[*Smiles insincerely.*]

## PEDRO MIGUEL COSTA
— I think about my mother from time to time.
Then my mind gets stuck on the moon.
And I think.
I wonder what it would be like to be at home now.
[*Sighs with longing*:
— And I think of my girlfriend. About Eva.
I think about proposing to her.
How long has it been, Eva?

That I looked into your gentle, loving eyes.
That rested on me. So gently. So full of love.
Brown, almond-shaped eyes.
As gentle as the Sado River.[30]
It's been far too long!
Almost like in another life. ---
I think about what it would be like
if we could live together.
You and me. Eva!
We'd have children together.
One of them would want to be a fireman.
That's what I wanted to be when I was little.
I wanted to save people's lives.
[*Thoughtful and serious*:
— But maybe
our sons
would rather prefer
to be policemen.
And serve the dictatorship. ---

[*Pause.*]

### PEDRO MIGUEL COSTA
— Make no mistake!
When I get out of here, my mother won't be
alive!
And Eva?
Eva wouldn't have waited for me!
That is, if I ever get out of here...
So I return from the moon.
Empty. Like my thoughts...

[*Pause.*]

## PEDRO MIGUEL COSTA

[*losing his mind*:

— And now --- I only think about my end.

How to end my life.

My life,

that isn't worth a damn here.

My life,

to which no door is open.

The whole lot has shut down.

[*Hallucinating*:

— Facing death ahead, ---

Seeing death,

face to face,

sensing death... ---

I can feel its cold breath now...

how it silences me!

[*Shudders with cold. Silence.*]

## PEDRO MIGUEL COSTA

— I am alone, in the midst of loneliness.

Time does not stop.

Does not stop ticking.

To tick.

Tick-tock

Tick-tock

That's another way to die.

Tock.

Nothing left for me

to pass the time.

To kill time!

Tick.

No book. No pen. --- --- Tock.

[*Grabs his hair and pulls it out*:
— I am surrounded by concrete and barbed wire. ---
I am far away from here,
with my thoughts.
So far. Far away from here.
But my thoughts stumble. About thoughts.
That I want to write down.
I want to sort them.
By size, weight, and color.
But I don't have any paper to hand.
No pen. --- Everything is pitch black.
So I write!
Rubbing my fingertips.
I write scraps of words on the wall.
On the rough, damp surface of the gray wall.
Words that rise from nothingness inside me.
Gain form. Become thoughts.
Until...
Until the blood runs from my fingertips.
My blood...
With which I write myself down.
I write;
dictate to myself:
I am no hero, Lord!
Please let this bitter cup pass me by!
Remove the thorns and thistles from my fate!
Remove the sting of death from my flesh!
My life is one day. Which must not be allowed to run
out like this. ---
[*Looks at his shaking hands, despairing*:
— I am so far away. From home.
From the truth. From life.

Every thought is like a heavy stone.
That falls to the ground.

[*Pulls a stone out of his trouser pocket and lets it fall to the ground with a deafening thud.*]

## PEDRO MIGUEL COSTA
— My gravestone.

[*He lets the carnation fall to the ground. Lowers his head. The light slowly goes out. He offers his hand to Ana Luísa Rebelo. Cláudio Pestana enters the stage. He also has a red carnation in his hand. He stands next to Pedro. The light brightens again until it falls completely on Cláudio.*]

## CLÁUDIO PESTANA
— My name is Cláudio Pestana.
[*Blushes*:
— Accused of passive homosexuality. ---
I always believed that the secret police only tortured people
to extort information.
To force confessions.
To punish perpetrators.
Or to frame the innocent for a crime.
To get rid of them...
But the PIDE also tortures,
because they enjoy
to torture.

[*Pause.*]

## CLÁUDIO PESTANA
— I had to take off my clothes.
The shirt. The trousers. Everything.
I stood naked in front of them.

In front of the policewomen, the female brigade of
the PIDE.
They aren't women!
They are monsters!
I tried to cover my shame with my hands.
But every time I covered my genitals,
I was slapped, slapped, once and again.

---

Flash! Flash!
They wouldn't stop taking photos of me.
Aiming at robbing me
of the last shred
of dignity.
Then they laughed.
And said they'd show it everywhere.
Even to my mother.
And they laughed heartily.
They laughed at me. Me. The ridiculous figure that
was standing there
in front of them in the dungeon.
And who tried in vain
to hide somewhere in the dark
from them and their mockery.
Then suddenly, on a whim,
they hit me.
Beat me up. Punched.
They hit me with their fists.
They kicked me.
They dug their knees into my stomach.
Beat me black and blue.
I could no longer feel my arms.

Not even my legs.
I could barely stand.
They continued to beat me wildly.
Hit me everywhere. On my face.
Hit my buttocks. My testicles. My back.
They tried to break my spine.
Until someone said: That's enough!
[*Moaning*:
— That's enough, yes? Please! That's enough! ---

[*Pause.*]

## CLÁUDIO PESTANA
— I walked crooked for a week.
Couldn't straighten up.
Couldn't stand up straight. ---

[*Pause.*]

## CLÁUDIO PESTANA
— They enjoy it:
To see me squirming on the floor.
How I rebel for a moment and then collapse.
How my lips burst,
how I bleed here and there,
after they hit me again,
full of glee,
thrust their truncheons into my guts.
They go on, on, on and on...
until they stifle the screams in my throat.
Until the scream is just a moan,
a gasp. [*Moans, gasps*:
— Until I cough up blood
and can no longer wriggle.

Then finally
they let go of me. Leave me
motionless, unconscious.

[*Pause.*]

## CLÁUDIO PESTANA
— Then, suddenly, they stand in my cell again.
They put a pistol to my temple.
Cock the hammer.
They play their antics with me.
Laughingly. Pretending. Then suddenly
they pull the trigger.
I flinch. Desperately.
I close my eyes in a flash. With fear.
My whole body trembles.
But they laugh again.
You were lucky; they sneer and jeer.
There was no bullet in it. This time!

[*Pause.*]

## CLÁUDIO PESTANA
— There they are again. Again and again.
There they are.
They show up very suddenly.
They shout. They yell at me.
Throwing insults at my head.
Degrading me to nothingness.
They have no sense of shame.
It is unfamiliar to these vile animals
to feel ashamed.
Their voices burn themselves into my soul.
Every word is like another slap in the face.

Another slap. In the face.
BAM – CRACK – SMASH!
"You gay pig!,"
Torture.
"Faggot!,"
Torture. Torture!
"Pansy!"
Torture.
"Son of a bitch!"
They say all sorts of things to me.
[*Covers his ears*:
— But they don't say my name.
[*Remembering*:
— Cláudio! ---
The son of a bitch!

[*Pause.*]

## CLÁUDIO PESTANA
— They deprived me of my sleep.
They wouldn't let me sleep.
For three days. And three whole nights.
They won't let me sleep.
I am so tired. I feel the need ---
to sleep. Sleep!
My eyelids are getting heavy.
My body is getting heavy.
I can no longer hold myself up.
I lose my sense of balance.
I lose all feeling.
My knees are shaking.
I am staggering.
Where am I? Where am I?

Who am I?
The body becomes weak.
My thoughts are empty.
I lose all sense of time.
I feel -- - dizzy.
Everything is spinning.
I'm going crazy. I'm going nuts.
Hallucinations. Hallucinations.
[*Shouting*:
— Is someone here?
Oh yes! There is.
It's me. Just me! --
I hear a whistle. Penetrating through the ears.
My head is splitting in two.
I have a terrible headache.
My muscles cramp up. Become paralyzed.
Paralyze the whole body.
Nothing holds it together. Yet, I am still upright.
I stumble.
My nervous system collapses.
I crash.
I fall.
Fall.
The floor opens up.
I fall in.
Fall...
I hit the ground terribly.
My God, where am I? ---
Almighty Father!
How far
have I fallen?

*[Pause.]*

## CLÁUDIO PESTANA
— They think it's fun...
*[He slaps his hands over his mouth*:
— No!
There are things that must not be said!
Things that should remain unsaid.
I won't say it here.
Everyone knows only too well what man is capable of.
When he is given authority over others.
When he is allowed to run roughshod over others.
Like a pack of wolves attacking a sheep. Tearing it
open.
You know only too well how much cruelty this
category of human being is capable of.
Yes, men can be bribed.
They let themselves be corrupted by the power,
which grows in their hands.
You know it! Only too well!
What they are capable of! --- These animals!

*[Pause.]*

## CLÁUDIO PESTANA
*[saddened*:
— They won't let me go to the toilet.
I have to go to the toilet.
They force me to hold out. Until I can't go any more.
But they won't let me go to the toilet.
I have to defecate on the floor.
In front of them all.
They stand around me.

Watch me.
They watch over my shoulder.
Starr.
And they are happy,
that I'm ashamed of them.
They hit me again.
Again, they make fun of me. About the worm.
--- Laughter.
Then they shout: You pig!
Then they order me to undress.
And wipe up the faeces and urine with my shirt and
trousers.
Then they order me, --- the pig, ---
to put the dirty, smelly clothes back on.
And they don't allow me to wash myself.
For days. I'm not allowed to wash!
It stinks. -- No!
It's me --- who stinks.

[*Pause.*]

## CLÁUDIO PESTANA

— Deep inside me slumbers a dream.
That sometimes wants to rise to the surface of my
consciousness.
I dream of seeing the clean beaches
of the Algarve[31] once again.
I dream of sitting on the beach at night.
And listening to the sea.
How the waves roar. Break. Foam.
I can hear it! The dead sea inside of me!
And I wash my hands in its flood.

The salty water encloses my body.
It also cleanses and purifies my thoughts.
The eternal sea that I miss so much,
drowns me, lovingly...

[*Pause.*]

## CLÁUDIO PESTANA
— No, I'm still alive.
The sea is far away. Far, far away.
They give me pills,
which I have to swallow.
My pupils dilate.
Absorb everything. The bars.
The door fits into my eye.
I am free. Free as a bird.
Crazy.
I have the strength to bend the bars
to bend them apart.
I can fly. Fly.
Over fields. Over the open sea.
Its roaring waves.
The wind whips my face.
The water is churned up by wild waves.
Then suddenly... there is no wind at all...
Surprisingly, it is as still as now...
And --- unexpectedly,
comes the plunge into the depths.
Everything crashes down on me.
The walls to the left, to the right,
the ceiling collapses on me and -- smashes -- me.
It's spinning.

Everything is spinning. I have to... vomit.
[*Vomits.*

### CLÁUDIO PESTANA
— Colors smudge. Run into each other.
Turn black. My eyes go black.
What are they doing to me?
They're driving me crazy.
They're killing me.
They're going to get me! [*Looks backwards in horror, but
there's no one there.*

### CLÁUDIO PESTANA
— They'll get me --- They'll destroy me. [*Cries. Screams.*

### CLÁUDIO PESTANA
— I don't take the drugs. I refuse to take them.
Put them down, they shout.
I fight back with my last ounce of strength.
I don't want them!
I don't want the stuff! No!
They punch and kick me,
until I swallow them.
[*Swallows*:
— Then ---
all of a sudden ---
the withdrawal. Of the drugs.
From one day to the next.
They laugh.
Laugh at me. Laugh at me again.
The gay pig.
The son of a bitch.
The faggot.

My body is shaking.
My whole body is shaking.
Sweating, weakness, nausea;
trembling... with fear ---
Give me the damn pills!
Give me all of them at once!
Then, it's finally --- finally, over!

[*He drops the carnation on the floor. Lowers his head. The light
slowly goes out. He takes Pedro Miguel Costa's hand. Rafael
Barros steps onto the stage. Like Ana Luísa Rebelo, he is dressed
all in white. He joins the three of them. The light switches on
again.*]

### RAFAEL EDUARDO BARROS
— My name is Rafael Eduardo Barros.
I'm a student at the Institute of Economics and
Finance at the Technical University of Lisbon.
I come from a destitute family.
I owe it to my mother that I am allowed to study.
She doesn't begrudge herself anything; she sacrifices
herself; she saves everything from her mouth;
to make my dreams possible.
The dream of a better life.
The dream that remained closed to my parents.

[*Rafael Barros looks at his hands.*]

### RAFAEL EDUARDO BARROS
— We wanted justice so badly.
And since there is no justice in this country,
we were ready to force it with our hands.
With our bare hands.
We took a PIDE informer into custody.

Manuel Fernandes e Castro.
Nobody else would have done it.
Nobody would have dared.
We interrogated him. For the sake of the truth. ---
The truth... And nothing but the truth.
We brought him before our court.
We passed judgement.
In the name of the Portuguese people...
We were just about to execute the sentence...
When suddenly the police burst in.
And suspended justice once again.
The executioner's servants protected him.
They arrested us like common criminals;
us,
who only wanted justice;
who only wanted a fair trial
a just sentence.
Suddenly, a shot rang out.
A shot and a scream.
A body fell, muffled, to the ground.
My body.
Because I panicked.
I wanted to escape.
Because I wanted to knock the gun
out of the policeman's hand,
who was pointing at my friends.
Absurd! I know.
The policeman pulled the trigger.
--- And so my body fell lifeless to the ground.
--- Nobody escapes.
No one escapes their fate!

And my predestination was
to breathe my last then and there. ---
Now I ask myself:
What was the point?
What did I die for?
What did I give my life for?
My future only lasted a moment.
Was about to be my past. ---

[*Pause.*]

## RAFAEL EDUARDO BARROS
— They continue to pass their laws.
Which only benefit the henchmen and the angels of
death.
No one else benefits from these laws,
which they pass with pomp.
They propagate these laws as the people's welfare.
But the people do not fit between the paragraphs of
repression,
of subjugation and suppression.
The people cannot breathe with the gag in their
mouths.
The paragraphs are formulated in such a way that
they suffocate the little man. Crush him.
Extinguish all life in him.
Where does that leave us, the unprotected?
By the wayside!
[*Thoughtfully, quotes from memory*:
— In this country, you die,
if you open your mouth!
In this country, you die,
even if you remain silent!

[*Decidedly*:
— So what do we have to lose?
Raise your voices in a sea of revocation!
Shout it from your souls!
And die with your heads held high!

[*Pause.*]

## RAFAEL EDUARDO BARROS
— There they go! There, they carry my coffin.
On their shoulders
they carry my mortal remains. ---

[*Pause.*]

## RAFAEL EDUARDO BARROS
— Dear friends! Dear parents!
[*He lays his hands on his heart*:
— I have received your prayers.
And I do thank you for your prayers. And
lamentations.
Your words to God have calmed me down.
They have quelled my hatred and pain.
Thank you! I am doing well!
I have arrived. At my destination.
God the almighty, benevolent, loving
has taken me in.
Just as he welcomes every righteous person into his
kingdom.
Everyone whose heart is in the right place.
Who is pure of heart.
I am compensated for my suffering by the love and
justice of God.
His love refreshes and strengthens me.

Blessed be the Lord!
And yet I am so unspeakably sad,
because I see you afflicted and saddened.
I see your gloom, your weariness.
To mourn a son...
To lose a friend...
To lose your freedom...
is probably the worst thing that can happen to you.

[*Pause.*]

## RAFAEL EDUARDO BARROS
— They censor us. They silence us.
They have declared our dreams, visions, and utopias
illegal.
They have used violence to
gag and shackle us.
They have raped the truth in courtrooms.
The truth that is offered no seat in court.
The truth that they fight to the death.
With their cheap tricks and their collusion.
Their judicial secrecy. --- Censorship.
I would like to remind you that the truth will one day
be rewritten.
But that's another story. ---
Here, in the kingdom of heaven, there is justice!
And it's defended with a naked sword of judgement.
A sword that can cut in two
a jet-black, enchanted heart
with a single, clean blow.
There is no one here,
who is more equal than anyone else. -

Ipse venena bibas!
Here, they will drink their own poison!
Here, the evil spell turns
against the sorcerer,
who conjured it upon us. -
Hellfire awaits you. ---
--- God alone is righteous! ---

## RAFAEL EDUARDO BARROS
[*groans:*
— There, they carry it away... My body. --- There!
--- They're carrying my coffin. On their shoulders.

[*The light goes out abruptly. All off.*]

# Third scene
## »Do not stop me... that I may go to my Lord!«
### (Genesis 24, 56)

*Hundreds of fellow students, a few courageous professors, friends, and family members, including, of course, Maria Amália Ramalhos, the mother of the deceased, have gathered in a small chapel. Undaunted, they have gathered to honor and to pay their last respects to the late Rafael Eduardo Barros. Many are standing outside. Smoking. Whispering. Mourning. A stained glass window is set into the wall. It shows the Archangel Michael with his shiny blue sword drawn from its scabbard. The devil lies at his feet, caught in his own manacles and in the delicate chains of the rosary, which are impossible for the demon to break on his own. The demonic creature's gaze begs for mercy. --- Everyone gathered here mourns Rafael Eduardo Barros, whose open coffin has been placed out in the chapel. The corpse lies frozen and cold in velvet. Rafael's hands have been lovingly folded on his chest in prayer. The face is pale and expressionless. To the left and right are two white, brightly lit candles and a large, beautiful wreath decorated with white flowers. The mother is praying. Only her lips are moving. Twitching slightly. Her voice remains silent. She is crying. Without wanting to, tears roll down her no longer young, oval face. Finally, as the ache becomes too painful, she takes out a handkerchief and holds it to her mouth. She uses it to stifle the involuntary cry. Someone taps her gently on the shoulder. She slowly turns around to face the person. She sees that it is one of the students. Who now gently takes her in his arms. He squeezes her briefly against his chest and then lets her go. He wants to tell her how sorry he is. How much they all, those who have found their way here, are enduring the cross of suffering with her. But there are no words to express it. He, too, remains silent. And hopes that the meager embrace might have been able to bring her some comfort after all. --- In the meantime, a man in plain clothes has joined the mourners. You can tell he must be a policeman. Because he's not wearing black. His face shows no sign of heartache. His eyes are icy. Fixed. But he observes closely how the mourners move. After the last prayer, someone blows out the candles. The coffin is closed. Now it has finally gone dark. The bearers lift the heavy, wooden coffin onto their shoulders and step out of the chapel. The mother wipes the tears from her eyes. She stands behind the coffin. Her legs tremble slightly. Outside, on both sides of the road, police officers and police dogs wait intimidatingly for the mourners. They take a few anxious steps. But suddenly, out of the unbearable silence, one of the students starts singing the Portuguese national anthem. Soon many, indeed almost all, voices have joined in the singing. Every note of the song gives them new courage. As the mourners sing the verse:* — Às Armas, Às Armas,[32] *one of them shouts:* — Death to the fascists! *Another shouts:* — Down with the PIDE! *The person picks up a stone from the ground and throws it at a security guard. But the riot police stand ready. They react with lightning speed. They unleash their full force. Armed with batons, they hit the funeral procession. They aim for heads. Even the mourners carrying the coffin are struck by force. The coffin falls to the ground. Some of the mourners are arrested. Others are bitten by the dogs. Nevertheless, the mourners continue to shout:* — Murderer, murderer!][33]

[*The lights go out again. Everyone leaves.*]

# Fourth scene

»Thou tellest my wanderings:
Put thou my tears into thy bottle:
Are they not in thy book?«
(Psalm 56, 8-9)

*Nothing happens for a while. Then Rafael Eduardo Barros steps onto the stage, searching. He stands next to his coffin, which is in the center of the stage. Shortly afterwards, the priest joins him.*

RAFAEL EDUARDO BARROS — Why isn't anyone standing around my grave? Where have they gone? Where are you all? I look around me. Desperately. Bitter. The graveyard is empty. Mother, I shout. Friends, comrades, where are you? Only a gravedigger and the priest have arrived in the meantime. The priest stands somewhat awkwardly in his black robe. He is standing. In front of me. Bends down. Towards me. Over me. Is here. With me. Close. And murmurs. Silently. Prays. Quietly. I pray with him. Still in pain. His voice sounds cool and cold. Impartial. Indifferent. Objective. He doesn't know me. He doesn't know my motives either. The father opens his liturgical book, bound in black leather. He finds the passage he is looking for. Now a gentle breeze tries to turn a new page.

PRIEST — And now says the Lord who created you: Fear not, for I have redeemed you; I have called you by name; you are mine! We give your body to the earth. -- Jesus Christ, who has risen from the dead, will raise you, our brother, to life.

85

**RAFAEL EDUARDO BARROS** — Now the gravedigger lowers my coffin.

**PRIEST** — I am the resurrection and the life. He who believes in me will live even if he dies, and everyone who lives and believes in me will never die.

**RAFAEL EDUARDO BARROS** — The servant of God sprinkles my coffin with consecrated water.

**PRIEST** — You were baptized in water and in the Holy Spirit. The Lord will complete in you what he began in baptism.

**RAFAEL EDUARDO BARROS** — Now he picks up a handful of earth from God's field. Even as he speaks, he throws it on the lid of my coffin.

**PRIEST** — From the earth you were taken, and to the earth you will return. But the Lord will raise you up!

**RAFAEL EDUARDO BARROS** — The priest mumbles as I speak softly, almost tearfully: earth to earth, ashes to ashes, dust to dust. --- He seems to have been waiting for me, because only now does he make the sign of the cross over my grave. And I too, still standing beside myself in confusion, cross myself. Full of reverence.

**PRIEST** — May Almighty God have mercy on you. Lord, grant him eternal rest, and let the eternal light shine upon him. Let him rest in peace!

**RAFAEL EDUARDO BARROS** — Once again, he draws the sign of the cross in the air.

**PRIEST** — Blessings from the Almighty and Merciful God, the Father, the Son, and the Holy Spirit.

**RAFAEL EDUARDO BARROS** — Together we pronounce the last word. Even if my voice no longer has any sound in this world.

**PRIEST** and **RAFAEL EDUARDO BARROS** [*together.* — Amen.

[*Curtain.*]

# Second farce

## First scene
»And the smoke of their torment
ascends forever and ever«
(Revelation 14:11)

[*Guilherme Vasconcelos is being held in a dungeon cell. There is a table next to him. It is dark and damp, and it smells of mold. Guilherme's head is lowered to his chest. He has been clearly mistreated. He is weak, and it takes him some time to speak. He has to breathe slowly between every word he utters. A body lies stretched out on the floor next to Guilherme. Screams can be heard from the neighboring dungeon cells, and here and there, a cry for mercy is perceptible. You can hear malicious laughter.*]

[*Two DGS agents enter through the prison door.*]

**FIRST AGENT** — It's time for you to sign your confession. [*Looks at the motionless body lying on the floor.* — What's wrong with him?

**SECOND AGENT** — He's a goner. The devil himself has taken him with him! He's probably had a heart attack. Our last conversation didn't go down too well with him. --

[*Laughs.*]

**FIRST AGENT** — You can tell by the stench! Leave him for another day or two. --- So that our friend here can get used to what awaits him soon.

[*Laughs again.*]

**GUILHERME VASCONCELOS** — Funny!

**SECOND AGENT** — Shut up, you piece of shit!

[*He punches Guilherme in the jaw, who gives a short yelp.*]

**SECOND AGENT** — You think you're really clever, don't you?

[*The first agent switches on the desk lamp. It's a harsh light. The second agent grabs Guilherme's hair. He pulls Guilherme's head by the hair until his eyes stare into the bright light.*]

**FIRST AGENT** — Let's go through the names of your friends together!

**GUILHERME VASCONCELOS** — I don't remember anything! I can't remember any names! --- Who? --- I have no friends!

**FIRST AGENT** — Oh no? Can't you? [*Sneers at his colleague:* — Did you hear that: he doesn't remember anything! [*To Guilherme:* — You're taking the piss, aren't you?

**GUILHERME VASCONCELOS** — That would never occur to me!

[*Enraged, the second agent beats Guilherme until he is bleeding from the mouth and nose.*]

**FIRST AGENT** — You're a Bolshevik, aren't you? What are the names of the others? We already know some of them. ---

[*Takes a piece of paper from the table and begins to read aloud.*]

**FIRST AGENT** — Marta Figueiredo, Júlio Oliveira, Rodrigo Veríssimo...

**GUILHERME VASCONCELOS** [*hastily*: — No! I don't know them. I don't know anything about them! They must be fascists!

[*Guilherme Vasconcelos spits on the floor. The second agent sees red. He lifts Guilherme out of the chair and throws him to the floor. He kicks Guilherme with all his might.*]

**SECOND AGENT** [*as he kicks*: — Who do you think you're talking to? You simpleton! What kind of manners are these to spit at my feet? Do you think you're here at home?

**FIRST AGENT** — That's enough! That's enough! He's had enough! Don't forget that he still has to appear in court!

**SECOND AGENT** — "Half a dozen strokes at the right time" never hurt anyone![34] By the way, I'm not afraid. Of the judge! He'd better watch out for us! There's only one person we have to answer to! Only one! To no one else!

[*He finally stops beating Guilherme, who has now lost consciousness. The light goes out.*]

[*Curtain.*]

# Second Scene
## »... and nothing but the truth«

*We are back in the same courtroom of the Tribunal da Boa Hora as in the first scene of the first farce. The light in the room is brighter than before because it is daytime. However, it is a cold light that falls on the stage. A framed picture of His Excellency, the late Prof. Dr. António de Oliveira Salazar, hangs on the wall just behind the judge's desk.*

[*A small group of people were allowed to attend the trial in the public seats of the courtroom. A man in a gray police uniform sits in the dock. The people in the audience are whispering to each other. Nobody laughs. Because there is no reason to laugh. The judge enters. He is a fat, unpleasant man. He is wearing a dark suit, a white tie, and a black robe. He is not wearing a blindfold and does not need a scale. The only thing at his side is the judge's sword, which he intends to use cruelly. Everyone suddenly falls silent. When the judge enters, everyone stands up. The judge is about to sit down when he notices the carnations that have been lying scattered on the floor near the edge of the stage since the second scene of the first farce. He goes to the carnations, tramples them, and wipes them off the stage with his feet. Then he finally sits down at the judge's desk. Everyone sits down. With the exception of the defendant.*]

JUDGE — Defendant, you may sit down!

[*The policeman, António João dos Ramos sits down.*]

JUDGE — At the end of this trial, it is up to me to make a decision in the case [*reads out*: — Rafael Eduardo Barros against the policeman António João dos Ramos. --- The deceased Rafael Eduardo Barros was the son of the widow Maria Amália Ramalhos. --- Rafael Eduardo Barros was twenty-two years old, a student at the Institute of Economics and Finance at the Technical University of Lisbon, and joined a criminal mob on April 10 of the current year. As it turned out, their intention was to convict and then lynch an innocent citizen, Manuel Fernandes e Castro, a civil servant. To this end, they kidnapped him and accused him of being an unofficial employee of the secret police for state security. --- ---

[*The judge takes off his reading glasses and places them on the table. He turns to the audience.*]

**JUDGE** — I have a duty to make it unmistakably clear that the rule of law cannot tolerate such violations! Thank God we have left the days of lynch law behind us! What's more, this act of vigilante justice was not about dispensing justice, but rather the opposite, namely committing a crime! All those who were involved in the conspiracy against Mr. Manuel Fernandes e Castro, as I would like to clearly state once again – an honest citizen – will be prosecuted in the foreseeable future, according to the procedures established by law, and sentenced to severe prison terms!

[*Wants to put his glasses back on to continue reading, but pauses again briefly.*]

**JUDGE** — This will serve as an example to all those who think they can take the law into their own hands. Thanks to the severity of the law, such cases will not be repeated in the future!

[*Puts his glasses on the end of his nose.*]

**JUDGE** — The police were informed at around 10 p.m. by the witness, Maria da Conceição Perestrelo, who was walking her dog at night and thus witnessed the kidnapping of Manuel Fernandes e Castro by pure chance and from a safe distance. She stated that she had observed two figures, which turned to a man: Manuel Fernandes e Castro; forcibly placed a potato sack on his head and beat him up in the most brutal manner. Until he stopped resisting. – The two criminals have already been duly identified and are currently in custody at Caxias Prison. – Mrs. Perestrelo further testified how the three men went into this courthouse. Here they joined a group of dissidents that wanted to make short work of Manuel Fernandes e Castro under the direction of a well-known agitator and enemy of the state, Guilherme Vasconcelos, a student at the Faculty of Law of the University of Lisbon. However, this was prevented in time by the courageous intervention of the police.

[*Addresses the defendant.*]

**JUDGE** — Mr. António Dos Ramos, I request that you tell us again what happened next!

**ANTÓNIO JOÃO DOS RAMOS** [*stands up*: — When we stormed the courtroom, I and my colleagues were abused and insulted in the worst possible way. We were physically attacked. The rebels tried to overpower us with punches and kicks. One of them even tried to threaten us with a knife. The dissidents cowardly grabbed me from behind and held me by the arms. However, I was able to free myself and pull my pistol, a Walther P38, 9-millimeter, out of my belt holster. I fired the gun into the air. A bullet must have gone astray and hit the student, Rafael Eduardo Barros, in the stomach.

JUDGE — That's right! – You may sit down again! – After examining and assessing the facts of the case, the court has no doubt that the police officer, Mr. António João dos Ramos, did not use excessive force, as has been maliciously alleged by the family of the student who died and various other witnesses. All these [*contemptuous*: — witnesses had participated in the kidnapping of Mr. Manuel Fernandes e Castro and thus made themselves liable to prosecution. In addition to kidnapping and attempted lynch law, they also have to answer for criminal association. Mr. António João dos Ramos was merely defending himself and rescuing an innocent citizen from the hands of terrorists! It was undoubtedly a fatal accident, but from my point of view, it is not to be regretted!

[*Some of those present in the audience begin to cough; others clear their throats. The judge looks at them sternly and continues to announce the verdict unimpressed.*]

JUDGE — An accident that is not to be regretted, since Rafael Eduardo Barros voluntarily joined this criminal group whose declared aim was to murder the victim, Manuel Fernandes e Castro! The police officer, António João dos Ramos, therefore defended his own life and that of the kidnapped man in self-defense! --- In view of the facts presented here, I now pronounce the verdict. --- Mr. António João dos Ramos, rise, please!

[*António João dos Ramos rises from his seat.*]

**JUDGE** — The police officer, António João dos Ramos, is to be acquitted of the charge of excessive use of force brought before this court! --- Maria Amália Ramalhos will be charged with the costs of the trial!

**MARIA AMÁLIA RAMALHOS** [*rises from her seat in the courtroom* — My son has died! And everyone knows why! Because he was a member of the banned and underground Marxist-Leninist student association! And because he presided in the name of this very student movement, the Committee of Anti-Colonial Resistance, whose meeting was violently broken up by the police. The police beat the students with truncheons! Some of them were even thrown out of the third-floor window by the police where the committee was meeting in the Faculty of Law at the University of Lisbon! Rafael was arrested along with other members of the committee and sentenced without being charged. He had already served time in Aljube[35] for taking part in a demonstration against the Vietnam War. The police knew him only too well. Even as a pupil at Camões Lyceum,[36] he had called on his classmates not to wear the uniforms of the fascist Portuguese youth[37] and to boycott their gatherings. His name had been on the PIDE's blacklist ever since. Since then, he has been constantly spied on and subjected to state arbitrariness and persecution! The police officer who has just been acquitted here did not fire warning shots into the air, as has been claimed and asserted here, but shot Rafael in the stomach at close range! We all know that this is what happened, and nothing else! This policeman is a murderer! And you, Your Honor, have just made yourself his accomplice! --- But your hour will come! You will have to answer to a higher judge! Before the Lord. Before God! --- God alone is just and righteous!

[*Pause.*]

**MARIA AMÁLIA RAMALHOS** [*directs her face heavenward:* — God of vengeance, dear Lord, God of vengeance, shine forth! Rise up, o judge of the earth, repay to the proud for their deeds! O Lord, how long shall the wicked exult? They pour out their arrogant words; all the evildoers boast. They crush your people, o Lord... But the Lord will not forsake his people; justice will return to the righteous. [*She points at the judge:* — The wicked band together against the life of the righteous and condemn the innocent to death, while those guilty are cleared. But the Lord has become my stronghold, and my God the rock of my refuge. He will bring back on them their iniquity and wipe them out for their wickedness; the Lord our God will wipe them out. -- [*Points again to the judge, but this time threateningly:* — You shall fear my God!

[*Those present in the courtroom audience protest. Some of them whistle and boo the judge. They continue to sit in their chairs and look at each other in defiance. They begin to stamp their feet on the floor. First, it's just one, then two, and then all of* them together. *The judge bangs his gavel hard on the table several times. He demands silence.*]

**JUDGE** [*beside himself with rage*: — Silence! -- Silence in the courtroom! I'll have the courtroom cleared! You must accept the verdict! Justice is being done here!

[*The audience in the courtroom does not stop stomping on the stage floor with the soles of their shoes.*]

**JUDGE** [*shouts loudly*: — Guards! Guards! I'll have the courtroom cleared!

[*The light slowly goes out. The stomping now becomes a march. Now you can also hear marching from outside. The forbidden song by Zeca Afonso, "Grândola, vila morena,"[38] which is about brotherhood and equality, can be heard as a signal song tuning from a radio. The armed forces occupy the streets and government buildings. The Carnation Revolution[39] is in full swing. The lights come back on. They are brighter than before. Warmer than before. Meanwhile, the audience in the courtroom has stood up. They continue to trudge on the wooden floor and have placed their hands on their hearts with pride and dignity, as if the song were the national anthem. Now the judge hesitates. He realizes that the wind has changed. He also puts his hand on his heart and acts as if he has always stood up for the democratic republic and freedom that will soon be proclaimed.[40] He even approaches the picture of António de Oliveira Salazar and hangs it off the wall.[41] He now turns to the theater audience. And bows, slightly opportunistically. To the people.*]

[*Curtain.*]

— *The End* —

# Fifteen points to the play

»God alone is righteous«

(Isaiah 45, 24)

1. This play is a "tragedy."
2. A "tragedy" in two "farces."
3. A "tragedy" is always disconcerting.
4. Every sentence passed in a dictatorship is a tragedy.
5. The despots and their paladins mask and disguise themselves.
6. As a result, common people misunderstand their intentions and identities.
7. As it generally happens in a "farce."
8. Only this "farce" is no laughing matter.
9. This kind of "courtroom farce" is tragic. It makes us weep and lament.
10. It is tragic and unjust to have to administer vigilante justice.
11. It is tragic to condemn an innocent man!
12. It is unjust to acquit a guilty person!
13. It is also tragic and unjust to imagine that justice can be bought.
14. As it happened so often during the dictatorship!
15. As it still happens every so often today! --- Or are there no more "farces" in democracy?

# Afterword
## »But of the tree of the knowledge of good and evil, thou shalt not eat of it«
### (Genesis 2, 17)

This year marks the 50 anniversary of the Carnation Revolution, which peacefully brought down the *Estado Novo*.

Fifty years have passed, in which often only a half-hearted reappraisal of the anti-democratic rule of Salazar and ultimately Caetano has been carried out.

Despite all the celebratory speeches that are repeatedly held on April 25, Portugal's national holiday, and in which attention is repeatedly drawn to the danger from the far-right – the radical populist movement, *Chega*,[42] made gains in the last elections in March of 2024. A total of 50 members of parliament from this EU-critical party now sit in the Assembly of the Republic. In 1926, the military dictatorship had to force its way into power. Today, fifty years after the fall of the *Estado Novo*, the people (i.e., over 1 million individuals, mostly young electors) are voluntarily voting for a right-wing, extremist party that no longer wants to play democracy by the book.

The longing for an authoritarian order, the partly understandable anger of the citizens towards our politicians, who no longer see themselves bound by electoral promises and seem to be repeatedly entangled in accusations of corruption, embarrassing nepotism, and other lobbyist scams, contribute to the fact that many people cast a protest vote.

But what does fascism, to which protest electors willingly give their vote, stand for? Precisely because the traces of fascism have been blurred by acute amnesia over the last fifty years, many young people who enjoy "the grace of late birth" are often no longer able to recognize historical, social, and political connections between then and now. This is certainly not only the case in Portugal. To counteract this, my book, originally published in Portuguese, has been translated into German and now into English. It's dedicated to coming to terms with the past of Portuguese fascism, but it also reads as a general warning and as a universal reminder. I hope to contribute with *Salazar's Angels of Death* to a constructive debate on fascism in Europe and around the world. Maybe, walking together through the trails of oppression in my play, we may better understand and overcome despotism, tyranny, and its outlined perils that will always linger in an authoritarian or totalitarian regime. Democracy might have many flaws, but the rule of the people is still far better than any other form of government we have experienced so far. Sir Winston Churchill expressed this belief in his famous quote, "Democracy is the worst form of government, except for all others."

Miguel Araújo Oliveira
Lisbon, 2024

# Notes

»I will answer thee, and shew thee
great and mighty things,
which thou knowest not...«
(Jeremia 33, 3)

---

[1] During the dictatorship, the *Tribunal da Boa Hora* was notorious for not granting the accused a fair trial. Many were innocently convicted without the right to a defense. Many lawyers were intimidated or blackmailed into abandoning their clients to their fate.

[2] The acronym PIDE stands for *Polícia Internacional e de Defesa do Estado* (International Police and State Protection). The PIDE was formed in 1945 on the model of Scotland Yard. It took over the function of the *Polícia de Vigilância e Defesa do Estado* (Police for Surveillance and State Protection, PVDE for short), which had been founded in 1933 and whose agents had been trained in the use of torture techniques by the GESTAPO, among others. Although the PVDE was disbanded in 1945, this did not mean that its agents returned to civilian life; rather, they were absorbed into the reorganized PIDE and continued to go about their brutal business, while the head of the PVDE, Captain Agostinho Lourenço, was appointed president of Interpol in 1956 on the recommendation of the British government. From 1945 onwards, the PIDE was authorized to gain access to private households without a search warrant, to carry out arbitrary seizures, arrests, and torture, and to install wiretaps. The secrecy of the correspondence did not apply to the PIDE. The PIDE was supported by a prudently established information network consisting of unofficial collaborators who spied on the population and reported opponents of the regime to the PIDE or handed them over to the organization.

[3] The Henrique Mendonça Palace is located in the *Rua* (street) Marquis de Fronteira and was built in 1909 by the Portuguese architect Miguel Ventura Terra. Dom Fernando José Costa Mascarenhas was the twelfth and penultimate Marquis de Fronteira. In 1989, he set up a foundation that has since been running its own cultural program dedicated to history, art, literature, and philosophy. The house can be visited on certain days.

[4] The censorship authorities in the country forbade the reading of communist writings, as they contradicted the socio-political worldview of the fascists. Some libraries, taking a considerable risk, loaned illegal copies of Lenin's books under his real name, Vladimir Ilyich Ulyanov, which was unknown to most people in Portugal, even at times to the censors themselves.

[5] The scene described here is based on the testimony of a contemporary witness whom the author was able to interview for his book in 2004. She recalled that in the early 1950s, one of her fellow students at the Classical University of Lisbon was suspected of being politically active against the regime. Because the two were friends, the witness was also put under surveillance, although there was no evidence against her. Her apartment was searched, as described in the dramatic text. The eyewitness was also deliberately made aware that she was under surveillance. She died on the island of Madeira in 2016 without ever knowing what had become of her friend.

[6] During the dictatorship, striking was strictly forbidden and punishable as a crime. Strikes were violently broken up by the riot police and resulted in draconian measures such as persecution, arrest, torture, and, in some cases, even the murder of the ringleaders.

[7] In the street (*Rua*) António Maria Cardoso, no. 18-26, was once the headquarters of the PIDE. After the fall of the regime, the building was renovated and converted into a residential complex. Many former victims and their descendants protested

against this redevelopment. They demanded the construction of a museum to commemorate the victims, but the city council at the time categorically rejected this and gave the green light for the construction of luxury apartments. The political refusal to commemorate the victims is exemplary of the often difficult process of coming to terms with the past and the prevailing culture of remembrance in Portugal, which until recently was tantamount to a repression of memory. For example, it is very regrettable, even shameful, that the recognition of the national hero Aristides de Sousa Mendes with the inclusion of an empty coffin in the national pantheon (the place where the honorable Portuguese who distinguished themselves during their lifetime find their final resting place) only took place in 2021, more than half a century after Sousa Mendes' death. Aristides de Sousa Mendes had already been awarded the honorary title of "Righteous Among the Nations" at the Yad Vashem Holocaust memorial in Jerusalem in 1966. In 1940, Sousa Mendes, who held the office of Portuguese Consul General in Bordeaux, began issuing visas to all those who applied to him without exception. The Portuguese visa guaranteed everyone (including many Jews and stateless persons) the unhindered departure from France via Spain to Portugal. In doing so, Sousa Mendes saved the lives of around 30,000 refugees, which is why he is often referred to as the "Portuguese Schindler." In doing so, the Consul General defied a decree by Salazar that forbade the issuing of visas to non-Portuguese. Sousa Mendes defended his decision by saying: "If I have to refuse to obey, I prefer to refuse to obey an order from man rather than an order from God." The "Consul of Bordeaux," as he is known today, was immediately and dishonorably dismissed from the diplomatic corps at the behest of Salazar and died penniless in Lisbon in 1954. In 1986, the *New York Times* published an article calling on the Portuguese government to posthumously rehabilitate Sousa Mendes. However, the restoration of his violated honor and rights would only be granted by the Portuguese parliament in 1988. In 1986, a few months after the article appeared in the *New York Times*, the then President of the Republic of Portugal, Mário Soares, awarded Aristides de Sousa Mendes the Officer's Cross of the Order of Liberty, an important but comparatively minor distinction. It was not until 1995, again under the presidency of the socialist Mário Soares, that Sousa Mendes received the second highest honor of the Order of Christ. Finally, the newly elected conservative President of the Republic, Marcelo Rebelo de Sousa, decided to honor Aristides de Sousa Mendes with the Grand Cross of the Order of Liberty in 2017 during a trip to the US. The majority of the Portuguese press celebrated the decision but pointed out in many articles that the various state tributes came several decades too late.

[8] *A bem da nação* ("for the good of the nation") was a Portuguese propaganda phrase that was often used by the state in official letters. It implied that the measures taken would have a positive effect and thus serve the good of the people.

[9] UNITA stands for *União Nacional para a Independência Total de Angola* (National Union for the Total Independence of Angola). The movement was founded in 1966 by Jonas Savimbi, among others, and set itself the goal of liberating Angola from Portuguese colonial rule by means of guerrilla warfare. Angola's independence was achieved in 1974. However, UNITA was not dissolved and continues to exist as a political party.

[10] FRELIMO stands for *Frente de Libertação de Moçambique* (Mozambique Liberation Front). The Front was founded in 1962 by Eduardo Mondlane and Samora Moisés Machel to organize armed resistance against the mother country, Portugal. Portugal only granted Mozambique its independence in 1975. Since then, FRELIMO has transformed itself from an initially Marxist party into a socialist party.

[11] *Colónia Penal do Tarrafal* was a penal colony on the island of Santiago in Cape Verde, which was founded in 1936 to remove members of the opposition, such as members of the communist and socialist movements, from the metropolis of Lisbon. The prison conditions were harsh, so the camp was quickly

nicknamed *Campo da morte lenta* (camp of slow death). Due to the lack of medical care, many prisoners died miserably from subtropical diseases such as malaria, but also from malnutrition and the consequences of the inhumane working conditions in the quarries. The camp director imitated the German concentration camps under Adolf Hitler, and it is said that he had his guards trained by torture specialists in the Dachau concentration camp. In the nineteen-sixties, the camp was renamed *Campo de Trabalho do Chão Bom* (Good Soil Labor Camp). From then until its liberation in 1974, supporters of the independence movements from the Portuguese territorial colonies were held prisoners in the camp.

[12] In fact, there were many cases in which innocent people were arrested. For example, when a bomb attack on Dr. António de Oliveira Salazar failed on July 4, 1937, a large number of people were taken into custody. The PIDE had to show quick success and was prepared to arrest and torture innocent people. Among the prisoners was the painter José Lopes da Silva, who was accused of being connected to the assassination attempt. Da Silva was mercilessly tortured. It is still unclear whether he died as a result of the torture or whether he took his own life out of despair in the cell. José Lopes da Silva was only 29 years old. After a more recent historical review of the assassination attempt, it is clear that José Lopes da Silva cannot be accused of any involvement.

[13] Quote from the dictator, Dr. António de Oliveira Salazar.

[14] Another quote from António de Oliveira Salazar.

[15] Quote attributed to Marcello Caetano, Salazar's successor in office (although it may be doubted that Caetano expressed himself exactly like that).

[16] Alluding to the quote by Marcello Caetano: "Without our overseas colonies, we are exposed to indigence, that is, we are dependent on the welfare of rich nations. So it is ridiculous to go on talking about national independence. For a nation on the

verge of turning into a little Switzerland, the revolution was the beginning of the end. Now all we have left is the sun, tourism, chronic poverty, and the remissions of our emigrants, but only as long as they last. We will now acquire raw materials from the powers that have incorporated them, at the price set by the big sellers. This is the price the Portuguese will have to pay for their illusions of freedom."

[17] The Portuguese currency of the time consisted of the *escudo*, which in turn was divided into *centavos*.

[18] The fortress of Peniche (*Forte de Peniche*) was built in 1558 during the reign of king Dom João III to protect the region against pirates. During the dictatorship, the fortress was converted into a high-security prison, where political opponents were taken and regularly tortured. After the fall of the regime, the fort was to be turned into a hotel. After a wave of protests and outrage among the population, politicians finally gave in. The fort was transformed into a national museum, which today commemorates the resistance.

[19] The *Armazéns do Chiado* is a well-known commercial center in Lisbon's old town district.

[20] *Prisão do Forte de Caxias* (Fortress Prison) is located in Oeiras and was built in 1879 as a defensive base. In the nineteen-sixties, the fort became a high-security prison where prisoners were tortured and interrogated. It is still a detention center today.

[21] DGS (*Direcção Geral de Segurança*) stands for General Directorate for State Security and was the institution that replaced the PIDE in 1969. In 1968, Marcello Caetano took over as dictator from Salazar, who had literally fallen off his chair and was never to recover from his fall. Caetano was well aware that the PIDE's reputation was poor. It was considered bloodthirsty by the population. Arbitrariness was the order of the day. To appease the people when he took office and to give the impression of a new "spring" (meaning that there would be more

freedom and the state would blossom again in terms of social policy), Caetano had the PIDE dissolved and the DGS set up as a secret police force in 1969. However, the PIDE agents were not replaced, but simply incorporated into the newly created DGS. The function of the DGS remained the same, as did its *modus operandi*. The population soon saw their hopes betrayed and preferred to continue calling the DGS the PIDE, as it had in fact remained the same institution. In the early nineteen-seventies, the agents of the DGS were then trained by the BND (*Bundesnachrichtendienst*/German Federal Intelligence Service) and the American CIA. Among other things, the CIA taught their Portuguese colleagues how to use the then fashionable drug LSD as an instrument of torture.

[22] *Salazarista*: term for the followers of Salazar.

[23] *Primavera marcelista* ("Marcelinist Spring"), a term circulated by fascist propaganda implying that there would be liberal reforms when Marcello Caetano came to power. The truth is, however, that Caetano neither abolished censorship nor did he really intend to renew the PIDE/DGS. Nor did Caetano intend to end the wars of independence in the colonies, which were much criticized by the population and internationally. Nor was he capable of overcoming the rampant economic crisis. In the end, all that remained of the hope for improvement that had been fanned by propaganda was bitter disappointment and anger at Caetano, who was accused of promising too much but doing nothing to make a real and lasting improvement to people's lives.

[24] *Estado Novo* (New State), also known as the Second Republic in the euphemistic jargon of national-fascist propaganda. The term stood for the authoritarian dictatorship that ruled Portugal from 1933 to 1974. Following a military coup in 1926, which ended the First Republic of Portugal (1910-1926), a provisional military dictatorship was established in the country. In 1930, Dr. António de Oliveira Salazar, Professor of Economics at the University of Coimbra, was summoned to Lisbon. He was offered

the position of Finance Minister of the country. Just two years later, Salazar took up the post of President of the Council (*Presidente do Conselho*) and drafted a new constitution, which was ratified in 1933, thus legitimizing a new form of government, the *Estado Novo*, in the long term. From then on, there was only one party, the *União Nacional* (National Union). All opposition groups had to be dissolved and banned. A secret state police [initially the PVDE (1933-1945), later the PIDE (1945-1969)] was founded as a means of repression. The press censorship that had already existed since the First Republic was extended, while freedom of expression was further restricted. In order to reduce the national debt, Salazar imposed strict austerity measures. The country's problems, such as the continuing acute poverty of the population and their illiteracy, were not addressed by the dictatorship. Many Portuguese emigrated to seek employment in other countries, such as France. From 1968 onwards, they also went to Germany. At the end of the nineteen-fifties, the country's colonies sought independence from the Portuguese motherland. Salazar decided to crush these movements militarily. In the mid-sixties of the twentieth century, various student movements protested not only against the high tuition fees but also against the colonial wars, as many of them did not want to go to war. The students demanded political rights such as freedom of assembly and the abolition of censorship. In 1968, Salazar literally fell from his chair. Shortly after his fall, he suffered a stroke and died in 1970. He was succeeded in office in 1968 by Marcello José das Neves Alves Caetano, until then a professor at the Faculty of Law at the University of Lisbon. As the population was increasingly dissatisfied with the political situation in the country, Marcello Caetano promised reforms, which were populistically celebrated as the "Marcelinist Spring." In 1969, Caetano had the PIDE dissolved and replaced by the DGS. However, the DGS was in no way different from the PIDE. The colonial wars, which were controversial among the population, went on. Censorship also continued. Disillusioned, Caetano was ousted from office on April 25, 1974. The Armed Forces Movement (*Movimento das*

*Forças Armadas*) deposed him. Caetano went into exile and lived in Rio de Janeiro until 1980. On October 26, 1980, Marcello Caetano died of a heart attack. He was buried in Rio. In the meantime, the third Portuguese Republic had been proclaimed, which was led by a provisional government until 1975, the year of the first free elections. In 1976, a new constitution came into force, which largely abolished censorship. The Portuguese colonies were also granted independence in the mid-nineteen-seventies.

[25] *Escudo*: Portuguese currency that first came into circulation in 1911 during the first Portuguese Republic (1910-1926) and was retained until 2002. At the beginning of the new millennium, the *escudo* was replaced by the euro.

[26] Some of the victims of the PIDE called their tormentors "*anjos da morte*": angels of death; others called them "*pássaros-da-morte*": birds of death.

[27] In 1961, two students were arrested and sentenced to seven years in prison for toasting to freedom with a glass of port wine in a café. The world reacted indignantly at the time. An English lawyer named Peter Benenson was so angry that he published an article entitled "The Forgotten Prisoners" in *The Observer* on May 28 of the same year. A French translation of the article appeared the same evening in *Le Monde*. In his article, Benenson called for people to write a polite but firm letter to the world's unjust regimes to express the outrage of the free world against the imprisonment of political prisoners. The letters should also call for the immediate and unconditional release of the prisoners. Benenson believed that international pressure could lead to an amnesty for the prisoners. Benenson thus initiated the founding of a human rights organization that is today known as Amnesty International. To this day, it is a tradition at Amnesty to celebrate successes such as the release of political prisoners with a glass of port and to celebrate freedom by toasting *à liberdade* (to freedom).

[28] The Tagus (*Tejo*) is the longest river that runs through both Spain and Portugal and flows into the Atlantic at Lisbon.

[29] "*A morte saiu à rua*" ("Death takes to the streets"), a song by Zeca Afonso, actually José Manuel Cerqueira Afonso dos Santos, which was released in 1972. Afonso wrote the protest song in memory of the Portuguese artist and sculptor José Dias Coelho, who was murdered by the PIDE in 1961 because of his communist views.

[30] The source of the Sado River lies in the Serra da Vigia. It flows into the Atlantic at Setúbal (near Lisbon).

[31] A region in the south of Portugal that enjoys great popularity among foreign and domestic tourists for its breathtaking coastal scenery and beaches.

[32] "To arms, to arms," a verse from the song "*A Portuguesa*," composed by Alfredo Keil in 1890. The lyrics were penned by Henrique Lopes de Mendonça. The First Republic officially declared the song the Portuguese national anthem in 1911. The verse itself dates from around 1890, when the British issued an ultimatum to the Portuguese, demanding that Portugal give up the African colonial territories located between Angola and Mozambique and hand them over to the British crown.

[33] This scene is based on various statements relating to the funeral of José António Ribeiro Santos, a student murdered by the DGS on October 12, 1972. A group of students had observed a man at the university who they assumed was a DGS informer. As a joke, the students called the DGS and told the authorities that they had locked up a man in a lecture hall because he seemed suspicious to them -- suspicious of belonging to the PIDE. Two armed DGS agents were then sent to the university. They demanded that the students withdraw and leave the man to them, whom they immediately tried to escort outside unharmed. One of the agents claimed to have felt intimidated by the number of students, and thus made use of his firearm. José António Ribeiro Santos was critically injured. Another student

was also hit by a bullet. Both were taken to the hospital, where 26-year-old Ribeiro Santos succumbed to his injuries. His funeral, which was attended by hundreds of students, was strictly supervised by the DGS, and in the end, when it threatened to take on the proportions of a manifestation, it was violently broken up. Today, a Lisbon street bears the name Ribeiro Santos.

[34] António de Oliveira Salazar's quote about police violence.

[35] *Prisão do Aljube* (from the Arabic *al-jubb*, meaning "well" or "cistern") was a notorious prison for political prisoners, who were often held in solitary confinement and in complete darkness. Since 2015, after a long political back and forth, the building has been transformed into a museum to commemorate the resistance.

[36] *Liceu Camões* a secondary school in Lisbon founded in 1902, is named after the famous Portuguese poet Luís Vaz de Camões (born around 1524, died around 1579), the author of the *Lusiades* (*Os Lusíadas*).

[37] The *mocidade portuguesa* (Portuguese Youth Organization) was founded in 1936 for boys and two years later also for girls. Just like the Hitler Youth (*Hitler Jugend*) and the League of German Girls (*Bund Deutscher Mädel*) under the Nazis and the *Balilla*, Mussolini's youth organization, the *mocidade portuguesa* set itself the goal of ideologically indoctrinating Portuguese youth, imposing the Catholic faith as well as the fascist view of fatherland and family.

[38] "*Grândola vila morena*" is probably Zeca Afonso's best-known song. The song was written in 1964, but could only be recorded in 1971 and only outside the country (in Hérouville, France). Many of Afonso's songs were already banned in his home country, and "*Grândola vila morena*" did not escape censorship either. He himself had been temporarily arrested by the PIDE. When his song was played on Radio *Renascença*, a radio station occupied by soldiers of the armed forces, on the night of April 24

– 25 1974, it signaled the beginning of the military coup, which brought down the dictatorship under Marcello Caetano without violence just a few hours later.

[39] From the night of April 24 to April 25, 1974, soldiers from the Armed Forces Movement (*Movimento das Forças Armadas*) organized a military coup that peacefully ended the dictatorship under Marcello Caetano. The revolution became known as the *Revolução dos cravos*, or Carnation Revolution, as the population, who welcomed the revolution, placed red carnations in the barrels of the soldiers' rifles to prevent a bloody uprising as far as possible. Shortly afterwards, a provisional government was established. The third republic was proclaimed and given a new democratic constitution in 1976. Censorship was abolished, and the colonies gained their independence.

[40] Unlike in postwar Germany, there was no questionnaire (*Fragebogen*) in Portugal. After World War II, "every German was supposed to make out a questionnaire known as the fragebogen. There were stiff jail penalties for lying on your fragebogen. If it turned out from your fragebogen that you'd been a member of the Nazi Party, you couldn't exercise any trade or profession. All you could do was pick and shovel work," John Dos Passos wrote in his chronicle *Century's Ebb*. With a few exceptions, the majority of Portuguese judges, police officers, university professors, and other civil servants remained in their posts after the overthrow of the dictatorship.

[41] This passage is based on a photo taken on April 26, 1974, by the photojournalist Eduardo Gageiro at the headquarters of the PIDE. The widely published photo shows a soldier of the Armed Forces Movement taking the picture of António de Oliveira Salazar from the wall.

[42] *Chega* (which literally means *that's enough*) is a Portuguese, conservative, nationalist, and right-wing party founded in 2019. By using populist rhetoric, the party harshly criticizes the

European Union and attacks ferociously the Portuguese democratic system.

https://migueloliveira.jimdofree.com/english